At first she couldn't believe her eyes.

8, 15, 22, 29, 36, 45.

Those were the numbers in the paper.

And those were the numbers on her ticket.

She stared at the numbers. Chill bumps broke out on her arms, and her heart began to pound.

Oh my God. Oh my God.

Her hands were shaking so badly, she could hardly hold on to the ticket. She couldn't believe it. And yet the proof was right there.

She was a winner!

Patricia Kay

is a *USA TODAY* bestselling author whose first mainstream novel was nominated for a RITA® Award by the Romance Writers of America. She has written more than forty novels of romance and women's fiction. She and her husband live in Houston, Texas, along with their eighteen-year-old cat, Phoebe, and have three children and three grandchildren. To learn more about her, go to her Web site, www.patriciakay.com.

THE **Next** NOVEL ™

PATRICIA KAY
Wish Come True

WISH COME TRUE

copyright © 2007 by Patricia A. Kay

i s b n - 1 3 : 9 7 8 - 0 - 3 7 3 - 8 8 1 2 9 - 1

i s b n - 1 0 :   0 - 3 7 3 - 8 8 1 2 9 - 0

TheNextNovel.com

 HARLEQUIN®

PRINTED IN U.S.A.

From the Author

Dear Reader,

I'll bet, at some time in your life, every single one of you has dreamed about winning lots of money. How else to explain the popularity of lotteries and quiz shows? So when my critique partner, Colleen Thompson, suggested to me that I should do a book about a woman who wins the Texas Lottery, I immediately loved the idea.

Wish Come True is the result. It was a truly fun book to write because I could indulge myself in those same fantasies, yet remain safely removed from the problems a sudden influx of multiple millions brings with it. And it does bring problems. In researching what's happened to past lottery winners, I discovered that many of them end up losing all their money. I didn't want that to happen to my heroine, but sometimes characters have minds of their own and they take the story in an unplanned direction. Kate was no exception.

By the time I'd finished the book, I deeply admired her and wished I could keep going to find out what would happen to her next. I hope, by the time you finish the book, you'll love her, too, and will have thoroughly enjoyed reading about her.

As always, I love to hear from my readers. Visit me at my Web site, www.patriciakay.com, and drop me a line. I promise to answer speedily. Until then, warmest wishes and happy reading!

Patricia Kay

This book is dedicated to the memory of one of the loveliest and most courageous young women I've ever had the privilege of knowing: Catherine René Kay-Richard, the mother of my grandson, Ryan, who lost her fight against colon cancer on June 26, 2006, at the age of forty. We'll never forget you, René.

Acknowledgments
Many, many thanks to my two loyal friends and readers Alaina Richardson and Colleen Thompson. What would I have done without you while writing this book? Your knowledge and love of all things related to horses was a Godsend. But what I especially appreciate is your unflagging enthusiasm for my work and the way you constantly cheer me on. You two are the best!

CHAPTER 1

"Why don't I just shoot myself?" Kate Bishop grimaced at her best friend.

"Better yet," Linda Farrell joked, "I'll shoot you, and your kids can collect on your insurance." Then she became serious. "I wish I could help you, Kate, but you know my circumstances."

Yes, Kate thought. She did. Linda's finances weren't in any better shape than Kate's. Linda had opened an exercise studio for women a year ago and was barely scraping by. In fact, she recently admitted to Kate that she'd allowed her credit card balances to get dangerously high. Kate knew the feeling. Her Visa card was just about maxed out. She did have a new MasterCard, but she didn't want to use it unless there was no alternative.

She sighed. "The ceiling mess is pretty much the last straw." Kate still couldn't believe it had happened. Apparently, her roof had a bad leak, and because of all the rain this part of Texas had been hit with in the past week, water had accumulated in the attic until the weight of it caused the family room ceiling to cave in the night before.

"I know," Linda said sympathetically. "What did the roofing company say?"

Kate sighed again. "They say I need a new roof. But that'll just be the beginning. I mean, the ceiling will have to be repaired, and the carpeting will need to be replaced. God knows how much the whole thing will cost. What I *do* know is that I can't afford to spend a dime."

Kate was divorced and had four children: nineteen-year-old twins and two younger daughters, sixteen and thirteen. She got monthly child support for the two younger children from her ex, but even combined with her salary, the total was barely enough to cover basic expenses. Like many families, Kate and the kids lived so close to the edge, they were constantly in danger of falling off.

Kate briefly considered asking her mother to lend her the money to put on the new roof and make the repairs to the house. But if she did, how would she pay the money back? And could she stand to be obligated to her mother? Wouldn't that give Harriet August license to become even more bossy and opinionated about Kate's life and choices? Most of which Harriet didn't approve of or agree with, anyway.

It was so hard to be alone. So hard to shoulder every burden. Kate missed having a partner. Since her divorce seven years ago, she'd rarely even dated. Who had the time or the energy?

"So what are you going to do?" Linda asked.

"I don't know. Today, I kept thinking about the root canal I need, and about the cost of my health insurance going up, and about—"

Linda frowned. "Your health insurance?"

"Didn't I tell you about that?"

"No."

"Dr. Holland told us last week that the insurance company has raised our premiums. Mine's going to cost $168 more a month."

Linda's mouth dropped open. "Oh, Kate. That's terrible!"

"Tell me about it." Wearily, Kate glanced up at the clock on the wall. It was almost nine-thirty. Erin, her youngest, who had spent the day with her dad, was supposed to be home at ten. Kate drained the last of the coffee in her mug, then walked over to the sink and rinsed it. She smiled at Linda, who still sat at her kitchen table. "I'm sorry about dumping on you."

"Hey, what're friends for? Besides, I do my share of dumping myself, don't I?"

Kate smiled crookedly. What would she do without Linda? "I've got to run. I need gas, and Erin'll be home in about twenty minutes." She waved goodbye and let herself out the back door.

As Kate drove to the discount gas station she always

used, she thought about moving. Cranbrook was a nice town and a good place to raise kids, but as in most small towns, there weren't many job opportunities. Kate's job as an office manager for the best doctor in the vicinity was probably one of the better positions available. Certainly, it paid more than she could make doing anything else.

Even if I were qualified to do anything else....

But just the thought of moving the family to Dallas or Houston or even Austin, which was only a ninety-minute drive from Cranbrook, made her feel sick. Her entire family lived in Cranbrook, and although moving farther from her mother probably wouldn't be a hardship, she would miss her two sisters terribly. Sure, they could be pains in the ass at times, but she loved them.

And Linda!

God, how could she even think about leaving Linda? She and Linda had been best friends since kindergarten.

And then there were the kids....

Tom and Tessa would probably view a move to one of the bigger cities as an advantage. But the twins were nineteen, and many of their high school friends were already away at college. So a move wouldn't be traumatic.

But Nicole was a junior in high school—at that stage in life where moving away from friends would be traumatic. And Erin would be terribly upset if they moved. She was close to her father and both sets of grandparents. She'd also formed a strong attachment to her three-year-old half brother, Luke.

Kate sighed deeply. Thinking about her seemingly insurmountable financial problems was giving her a headache. As she pulled into the gas station, she decided that, like Scarlett O'Hara, she would put the problem on the back burner and deal with it tomorrow.

After filling the tank, she walked inside the station to pay for her gas. Standing there at the counter while the clerk finished waiting on a previous customer, Kate idly read the sign advertising the lottery jackpot, which was up to seventy million now.

"That'll be $25.60," the clerk said.

"Oh, I'm sorry," Kate said. "I was daydreaming." She handed the clerk a twenty and a ten.

"You want a lottery ticket?"

Kate never wasted money on lottery tickets. But for some reason, tonight she said, "Sure. I'll take three quick picks."

The clerk smiled and rang up her sale. Kate tucked the lottery tickets and her change into her purse and left.

Five minutes later, she was pulling into the driveway of her thirty-three-year-old, four-bedroom ranch house. Remembering the mess waiting there, she felt like crying.

Stop that. Didn't you tell yourself you wouldn't think about it again tonight? Now get a grip. Erin'll be home soon, and the last thing you want is for her to start worrying, too....

When Kate let herself in the back door, Ginger, their chocolate lab, bounded toward her, tail wagging madly. Kate leaned down and let the dog give her a few welcoming licks.

A few minutes later, Taffy, their orange cat of questionable origin, entered the kitchen. She stopped and stared with disdain at Ginger's antics. Kate couldn't help smiling. Taffy was so sure of her superiority in the world. Must be nice to have all that self-confidence.

Kate had just finished putting food into the animals' bowls when she heard a car door slam. A moment later, Erin blew into the kitchen like a whirlwind. Ginger, torn between the food and her favorite of all the kids, finally rushed over to give Erin a sloppy kiss.

"Hi, honey," Kate said. "Did you have a fun day?"

"Uh-huh," Erin said, green eyes shining. She pushed her glasses up; they were always falling down on her nose. "Mom, Luke is soooo smart. I taught him how to play checkers today!"

"You did?"

"Uh-huh. And during one game, he almost beat me!"

Kate doubted the three-year-old had the reasoning capacity to beat Erin at anything, but she didn't contradict her youngest. She continued to listen as Erin expounded on her day with her dad and his new family and tried not to feel resentful when Erin said, "Oh, and Mom, Dad said to ask you if I can go to Disney World with them this summer."

Disney World.

And Kate couldn't even afford a weekend in San Antonio. "If your father really *does* go to Disney World, and if the trip doesn't interfere with anything else you have planned, then of course you can go."

Erin grinned and threw her arms around Kate. "Thanks, Mom."

Kate hoped Mark wouldn't let Erin down again. Other plans had been made in the past that had never come to fruition. But she decided not to say anything right now to dampen Erin's happiness. Time enough if Mark reneged. Besides, why was it always Kate's responsibility to prepare her daughter for disappointment? In fact, she was heartily sick of always being the bad guy who pointed out reality whereas their father always seemed to manage to escape unscathed.

Erin walked over the refrigerator and opened it. "Is there any more pie?"

"No, sorry, honey, Tom finished it off before he went out."

"I'm hungry. What can I eat?"

"Oh, you're always hungry." Kate eyed her daughter's skinny frame and remembered when she, too, could eat anything and everything and never gain an ounce. Those days were long gone, she thought ruefully, looking down at her hips. "Have a banana."

Erin frowned. "I don't want a banana. Can I have some ice cream?"

"I'm not sure there's any of that left, either." Kate should have gone grocery shopping today, but after the roofing company rep had delivered his bad news, she hadn't been in the mood to do anything. Especially anything that cost money. "How about some hot chocolate with marshmallows?"

Erin made a face, but she obediently opened the pantry and extracted the box of hot chocolate packets.

"Get out the bag of cookies, too," Kate said, suddenly hungry herself.

The two of them had just finished their hot chocolate and cookies when Nicole, who had gone to the movies with some friends, came home, followed two minutes later by Tessa, who'd just gotten off work.

Nicole barely mumbled "hi" before heading off to her room, but Tessa, long past teenage moodiness, sat down at the kitchen table and reached for a cookie. "Mom," she said, "Tom and I were talking..."

Kate looked up.

"And he said he thought he could get some extra hours if he asked, and I know I could get an extra shift every week, so between us, I think we could pay for the new roof."

The tears that had been so close to the surface all day filled Kate's eyes. "Oh, Tessa," she said in a shaky voice. "I don't want you kids to have to take on more work. You've both got enough on your plate."

"But, Mom, we *want* to help." Tessa's blue eyes were earnest.

Sometimes Kate wondered what she had ever done to deserve such good kids. None of them had ever given her any trouble, whereas everyone she knew seemed to have some kind of serious problem with one or more of their children. "I know you do, honey," she said softly, "and it means more to me than I can say that you're willing, but you and Tom work hard enough as it is. And you've got school, as well. I don't want you to worry about this. We'll manage. We always do, don't we?"

After a moment, Tessa nodded.

Later, as Kate was brushing her teeth in preparation for bed, she realized that no matter how bleak things were financially, she was rich beyond her dreams with her kids.

The rain had finally stopped and a watery winter sun shone through the stained-glass windows of the First Methodist Church of Cranbrook at the end of the nine-thirty service the next morning. The choir was singing the last verse of "Come, Ye Faithful, Raise the Strain." Nicole, a soprano, looked angelic in her creamy choir robe. Kate fancied she heard her daughter's voice above the others as they sang:

Alleluia! now we cry to our King immortal,
Who, triumphant, burst the bars of the tomb's dark portal;

Alleluia! with the Son, God the Father praising,
Alleluia! yet again to the Spirit raising.

When the hymn was over, people began gathering
their belongings and slowly filing out of the church.

Kate and Erin stood, then joined the throng. They
walked outside into the crisp forty-degree air, and Kate
looked around, spying her mother and sister Joanna,
who were talking with Dolly Nickson, Joanna's best
friend. "There's Gran and Aunt Joanna," Kate said to
Erin. "Let's go over while we wait for Nicole."

"I wonder if it's someone from Cranbrook," Dolly
was saying excitedly as Kate and Erin approached.

"Must be," Joanna said. She looked at Kate. "Good
morning."

"'Morning," Kate said.

"Why do you say, must be?" Dolly asked.

"Because the Stop & Shop isn't exactly on a
highway or anything," Joanna said. "It has to be
someone local." She brushed imaginary lint from her
immaculate black wool suit. Kate's older sister always
looked as if she had just stepped out of the pages of
Vogue.

*And she has the credit card bills to attest to her fondness
for expensive clothes*, Kate thought.

"All I can say is," Dolly said, "whoever it is sure is a
lucky son of a gun."

"What're you talking about?" Kate asked.

"Someone who bought a lottery ticket at the Stop & Shop on Fifth Street won," Kate's mother said. She tousled Erin's hair. "Haven't seen you lately, sugar."

"I was at Dad's yesterday," Erin said.

"Yes, your mom told me." Harriet looked at Kate. "Where are Tom and Tessa this morning?"

"Tessa worked till ten last night and Tom was out late, so I let them sleep in this morning." Kate wished her mother's obvious disapproval of her parenting didn't always manage to put her on the defensive.

Harriet didn't comment, but her cool expression told Kate exactly what she was thinking.

"Wonder how much they'll actually *get*?" Dolly said to Joanna. She was obviously still talking about the lottery.

Joanna shrugged. "Half? The IRS takes a big cut. Maybe even less than half."

"Still," Dolly said, "even if it's only twenty-five million, that's a *fortune*." Then she giggled. "*Only* twenty-five million. Listen to me."

Kate bit back a smile. Giggling wasn't an attractive trait for a fiftysomething woman. But Dolly had been dubbed "Cutest Senior Girl" in her high school yearbook, and she'd never gotten past the designation.

Joanna turned her attention to Kate. "Mel told me about the roof." She was referring to their other sister, Melissa.

Kate made a face. "I'm trying not to think about it."

"What?" her mother said, frowning.

"Our den ceiling fell in," Erin said. "There's a *huge* hole where the ceiling used to be."

Harriet looked at Kate.

Kate explained, trying for matter-of-fact rather than poor-me.

"Just what you need," her mother said, shaking her head. "Can't the roof be repaired?"

Kate shook her head. "Charlie Wiggins says not." She didn't elaborate. She didn't want to talk about the roof. Not here and not now.

Just then Nicole joined them, and after she'd greeted everyone, Kate said, "Well, we've got to be going. I've a million things to do today, and Nicole has a special chorus practice at school, don't you, hon?"

"Yes, at two o'clock," Nicole said.

Kate leaned over and kissed her mother's cheek. "Bye, Mom. Bye, Joanna. Dolly."

Kate knew her mother wanted to say something more, but she didn't, and for that, Kate was grateful. Sometimes her mother could be insensitive, but today she seemed more in tune to Kate's mood.

Later that afternoon, with the kids all occupied with their own pursuits, Kate finally had a chance to sit down and really take stock of her financial status. She seriously considered just charging the cost of the new roof and other repairs to her MasterCard, but the thought of that much debt and how long it would take her to pay it off frightened her.

She couldn't believe it. And yet, the proof was right there. The numbers on her ticket matched the numbers in the paper. There was no doubt. She had won millions of dollars.

She walked back to her bedroom in a daze. When she got there, she sat on the edge of her bed and stared into space. Her hands were still shaking.

Calm down, calm down....

What should she do? She thought about the kids. Should she tell them? Tom was asleep. He had to be at work at seven. Tessa was probably still doing homework. Nicole would be listening to music and reading. Erin would be snuggled in bed with both Ginger and Taffy, maybe already halfway asleep. If she told the kids, they'd be too wound up to sleep and everyone would be exhausted tomorrow.

But she had to tell *somebody* or she'd burst.

Linda.

She'd tell Linda.

Kate laughed out loud. Linda would go ballistic.

She got up and headed for the phone, then decided to drive over to Linda's house instead. But before she left, she'd better find a good place to hide her ticket so it would be safe, because she wasn't going to carry it around with her. No way.

She looked around. Her jewelry box? No, too obvious. In her lingerie drawer? First place a thief would look. She finally settled for putting the ticket under her mattress.

Ten minutes later, she'd said goodbye to the kids, told them she wouldn't be gone long and was on her way.

All the way there, she kept pinching herself to make sure she wasn't dreaming.

CHAPTER 2

Kate was glad Linda only lived eight blocks away. In the state she was in, she wouldn't have wanted to drive very far. She was also glad she hadn't called Linda first. It was going to be a lot more fun to surprise her.

She knew Linda would be there because the two of them had talked earlier in the day and Linda had mentioned that she had to work on her receivables that evening.

"That's the worst part of owning your own business," she'd complained. "Getting people to pay you what they owe you."

"You need to set up something where their monthly fee is automatically taken out of their bank account," Kate suggested.

"I know," Linda had said with a sigh, "but everything I want to do costs money. And that's in short supply right now."

When Kate pulled into Linda's driveway, she saw light spilling out from the kitchen window, so she went to the back door and knocked.

Linda turned on the back light and looked startled to see Kate standing there. Her smile was quizzical when she opened the door.

"Surprised?" Kate said, hugging her delicious knowledge to herself.

"What's going on? Did something happen?"

"You could say that."

"Should I put on the coffee?"

"I don't suppose you've got a bottle of champagne."

Linda stared at her. "Champagne? Is somebody getting married or something? Have you been holding out on me?"

Kate just laughed. Oh, this was fun! "How about wine?"

"As a matter of fact, I've got some nice Reisling chilling in the fridge."

"Perfect." Kate plopped down at the kitchen table. "Put it in your best crystal. We've got something to celebrate." She could see Linda was dying to ask questions, but she obediently went into the dining room and came back with two crystal champagne flutes.

"We can pretend it's bubbly," she said, smiling.

Kate waited until they had their wine and had taken their first sip before she said, "I'm really glad you're sitting down, because when I tell you what's happened, you won't believe it."

"*What*, for heaven's sake? Is your *mother* getting married?"

Kate laughed again. "Nothing like that."

"If you don't tell me right this minute, I'm going to strangle you."

Kate took a deep breath. "Did you hear about someone from Cranbrook winning the lottery?"

"Yeah, they were talking about it at Mass this morning, but—" She stopped. Stared at Kate. "No," she breathed.

Kate nodded. "Yes."

Linda's mouth dropped open. "*You! You won the lottery?*"

"Yes." Kate couldn't stop smiling.

"Oh, my God."

"That's what I said."

"Kate! I—I can't believe it. Seventy *million?*"

"Well, it won't be that much when they get done, but—"

"Oh, my God, Kate, it'll still be *millions and millions of dollars!*"

Kate nodded, grinning. She was almost afraid to think about the money. It was simply too much—almost unbelievable.

Linda jumped up and grabbed Kate's hands. "How can you just *sit* there? You're a *millionaire!*" So saying, she pulled Kate up and twirled her around the room. They were both laughing like fools.

When they finally sat down again, out of breath and weak from laughing and shrieking, Linda said, "Think what this means, Kate. You'll never have to worry about money again. Omigod, I'm so happy for you. Of course, I'm also so jealous I could cry."

"Hey, you've been my best and dearest friend my entire life. You're going to share in this, too, you know."

"I *am?*"

"Of course. You know that building you're paying too much rent for? We're going to buy it. And those credit cards? Say goodbye to the balances. You're also getting a new car, whatever you want." She grinned. "Within reason, of course."

"Oh, Kate," Linda squealed. "Do you mean it?"

"Wouldn't you do the same for me if our roles were reversed?"

"Well, of course, but—"

"But what?"

"I don't know. I guess I still just can't believe this is true."

"I know. I'm still in a state of shock myself. Listen, can you get Sharon to work for you tomorrow?" Sharon was Linda's assistant.

"Probably. Why?"

"I want you to drive up to Austin with me. I have to go to the Lottery Commission to claim the money, and I'm too nervous to go by myself."

"You wouldn't rather have your mother or one of your sisters?"

"No. I want you. In fact, I don't plan to tell them

about this until after I go to Austin. I haven't even told the kids. You're the first one."

"I'm honored, and I'd love to go. In fact, I'll go call Sharon right now."

Ten minutes later, Linda came back to the kitchen, poured both of them more wine, and said, "Sharon was curious about where I was going."

"What did you tell her?"

"Just that I had some business to take care of. What're you going to tell Doc Holland?"

"I'll tell him the same thing."

"I just thought of something. You'll probably quit that job, won't you?"

"I don't know. I haven't thought that far ahead."

"With that much money, you won't need to work."

"That's true, but I have to do something. I'm not the lady of leisure type."

"Oh, Kate. You can do *anything*. Think of it. Buy a business. Do good works. Go to college. The whole world will be open to you. And the kids. Have you thought about what you'll be able to do for the kids now?" Linda's eyes were shining. "Tessa will be able to go to that design school in Rhode Island, the one she talks about all the time. And you can send Tom to flight school. You could even afford to buy him his own plane."

Kate grinned. She couldn't help but think about how she'd told herself last night that she was one of the luckiest people in the world, and that was before she'd won the lottery. And what Linda had just said, and the way she'd said it, drove home the point. Linda really *was* thrilled for her, almost as thrilled as if she'd won all that money herself. She was the best friend anyone could ever have. "I'm still too stunned to think rationally," Kate admitted. "It's just too big to comprehend yet."

"Don't worry. I'll help you comprehend."

Kate laughed. "You mean you'll help me spend."

Linda laughed, too. "What time do you want to go tomorrow?"

"Let's leave early. The kids will be gone to school by seven forty-five."

"If we leave that early, we'll hit some of the morning rush-hour traffic."

"Maybe we should wait until closer to nine, then."

"How about eight-thirty? I'll drive."

"Okay. I'll pay for the gas. And for lunch afterward."

Linda leaned over and hugged her. "And I'll let you."

The first thing Kate did when she got home was to check that the winning ticket was still under the mattress, even though she felt foolish doing it. Where else would it be?

After assuring herself the ticket was still safe, she checked on the kids.

All four were asleep. She stood for a long time in the

doorway of each room. Tomorrow everything was going to change, not just for her, but for the kids, and for her entire family. In some ways, the changes frightened Kate. That much money was a huge responsibility. And she'd heard some of the horror stories about how winning the lottery had ruined people's lives. But that wouldn't happen to her. She was a sensible person with a stable family. Still, the thought of all the coming changes was scary as well as exciting.

Although Kate was worn out, she knew she wouldn't sleep. Grabbing a comforter from her linen closet, she curled up on the sofa in the family room and stared at the ceiling where Tom had nailed a large piece of oil cloth to cover the gaping hole. She couldn't help smiling. Now she could get the roof fixed. Heck, she could get a new roof if she wanted.

I'm rich, she thought jubilantly. It was still so hard to believe. She kept wanting to get up off the sofa and go check the numbers on her lottery ticket again.

Eventually, her eyes closed and she dozed until five, when she figured it wasn't too early to get up. She quickly showered and was dressed before Tom came downstairs at six.

"Gee, Mom," he said, "you didn't have to get up. I coulda made my own breakfast." His dark hair was still wet from the shower.

"I felt like making you an omelette." She smiled at him. "I've also packed your lunch."

His answering smile warmed her heart. She knew mothers weren't supposed to have favorites, but she'd always had a special soft spot for her only son.

While he was eating, she woke the three girls—Tessa had class at the community college today, so she needed to get up early, too—then fixed their breakfasts and saw them off to school.

Erin was the last to leave. Kate watched her walk to the corner where she'd catch the school bus. Although Erin was thirteen now, she still looked like a kid to Kate, with her dark ponytail swinging, and her heavy backpack weighing down her five-foot-two frame.

My baby, Kate thought with a lump in her throat. It wouldn't be long before Erin would be gone. Next year she'd be a freshman in high school, and after she graduated she wanted to go to Texas A&M and study to be a veterinarian.

And the money Kate had won would make it possible. It would make everything possible.

Kate sighed and slowly walked back to the kitchen, where she poured herself a final cup of coffee. Kate drank her coffee standing up. When the clock read eight, she called Dr. Holland's office and spoke to Darcy, Dr. Holland's nurse.

"I hope everything is all right," Darcy said when Kate explained she had an urgent family matter she had to take care of and wouldn't be in.

"I should be there tomorrow," Kate said. She knew

Darcy was torn between curiosity and concern, but she didn't elaborate further.

As soon as they hung up, Kate called the roofing company and left a message saying she wanted them to put her on the schedule for a new roof.

Twenty minutes later, lottery ticket securely tucked into her wallet, Kate climbed into Linda's Toyota. Grinning at each other, they headed off to Austin.

They arrived at the Texas Lottery Commission Office on Sixth Street a little after ten. When Kate identified herself as the lottery winner of Saturday's drawing, the receptionist jumped up and said she'd get the director.

The ticket had to be authenticated, and Kate had to fill out and sign several forms, but by noon, she was presented with a ceremonial check for twenty-eight million dollars—the cash option less the initial cut to the IRS—and her picture was taken with lottery officials. She was assured that the money would be wired to her bank the following day and given a pamphlet that had been specially prepared for lottery winners.

The two women were giddy as they left the building.

"Where do you want to go for lunch?" Kate asked.

"The Shoreline Grill," Linda said with no hesitation.

Kate grinned. The Shoreline Grill was one of the nicest restaurants in downtown Austin. "Perfect."

Thirty minutes later, they were seated at a window

table, one that afforded them a dazzling view of the Colorado River, and a solicitous waiter was recommending specialties of the house.

They lingered over lunch, savoring prime rib and succulent crab cakes and indulging in a couple of the restaurant's famed margaritas. They even said the heck with their diets and ordered Vanilla Bean Crème Brûlée to have with their coffee.

It was two-thirty before they finally left the restaurant. Kate would have liked to go shopping, maybe treat both herself and Linda to a beautiful new outfit, but she didn't want to get home too late because she didn't want to have to explain to the kids why she hadn't been at work today. She planned to tell them about the lottery win tonight, but she wanted her entire family gathered together when she did it.

On the way home, she dug out the pamphlet she'd been given by the lottery officials and began to read it. One thing gave her pause. It was a warning about what would happen as soon as her win was made public. Kate grimaced. "Listen to this," she said to Linda. "It says here that I might want to get a new, unlisted phone number. Apparently people you don't even know start pestering you once they find out you've won the lottery."

Linda nodded thoughtfully. "That sounds like a good idea. In fact, I've heard about people who win a lot of money who have to hire bodyguards and put in sophisticated security systems."

"*Bodyguards?*" Kate said. She was astounded.

The more she read, the more she realized her life was going to change even more drastically than she'd imagined. Still, she could hardly believe some of the things the pamphlet warned against. For instance, she couldn't imagine her family turning hostile toward her, as some lottery winners' families had.

"This is horrible," she said, reading aloud to Linda. "This one man, when he won? His wife tried to poison him so she'd have all the money. And another one gambled it all away. Still another fell for some kind of real estate and investment scam and lost most of it."

"Well, you don't have a wife," Linda said, laughing. "*Or* a husband, and you don't gamble, and I can't imagine you being gullible enough to fall for any kind of scam."

"I know, but the way this sounds, it's like no one is happy after they win the money."

"I'm sure lottery officials feel they have to give you the worst-case scenario, just in case."

Some of Kate's excitement had segued into trepidation as she realized just what might be in store for her. "They advise consulting a financial advisor before doing anything with the money."

"That sounds sensible."

"But I don't know any financial advisors. I can't just look in the phone book, can I?"

"Talk to Ward McAndrews. He can probably recommend someone good."

Ward McAndrews was president of the First National Bank of Cranbrook, where Kate had her account. "He'll probably just want me to keep all the money in his bank."

Linda chuckled. "Yes, but even he's smart enough to know that's not gonna happen."

Kate sighed. She could see the days ahead were going to be filled with problems to solve and decisions to be made.

When they arrived at Kate's house, Kate hugged Linda goodbye, saying, "Since we couldn't go shopping today, I want you to keep Saturday free."

Linda smiled. "I will. You going to tell the kids tonight?"

"Yes. In fact, I'm going to call a family meeting and tell everyone at the same time."

"Oh, I'd love to be a fly on the wall and see their faces."

Kate grinned. "I *am* looking forward to it."

It was after five before all four children were home, and Kate, after calling her sisters and asking them to meet her at their mother's house at seven o'clock, told the kids she was ordering a pizza, after which they were going to their grandmother's for a family meeting.

"Mom," Tessa protested, "I can't go. I have to have my portfolio ready to hand in on Friday. And I'm working tomorrow and Wednesday nights."

"I have too much homework," Nicole complained. "Can't you just tell me what it's about afterward?"

Even Erin whined that she didn't want to go because she had to study for a math test, but Kate insisted. "I'm not asking," she said. "I'm telling you. I have something very important to tell everyone, and I want you to be there."

Tom gave her a strange look. "If you were dating, I'd ask if you were planning on getting married again or something."

Kate laughed. "You're not even close."

"We're not *moving*, are we?" Nicole said in alarm.

"No, we're not moving. Now stop guessing. You'll find out soon enough." Kate was too happy to get mad at them and ignored their continued grumbling.

At seven o'clock, with her family gathered around her, Kate took a deep breath and said, "I wanted everyone to hear this at the same time. I have some really fantastic news." She looked around the room, at all the dear and familiar faces all looking at her expectantly. "I won Saturday's lottery."

Her announcement was met with shocked silence. Then Joanna laughed. "Is this some kind of joke?"

Kate shook her head. "No. I'm perfectly serious. I'm the one who bought the winning ticket at the Stop & Shop. Linda went with me today to the lottery commission office in Austin, and they authenticated my ticket." She took the ceremonial check out of her purse and held it up. "Tomorrow twenty-eight million dollars will be deposited in my account at the bank. And also, tomorrow my picture is going to be in the paper with the official announcement."

Her mother looked as if she might faint, her sister Melissa gasped, Joanna stared and the kids started dancing around, shouting, "We're rich! We're rich!"

"Did you know when we were at church yesterday?" Joanna asked when the initial commotion died down.

"No, of course not. Do you think I would have been that calm if I had?" Kate said. "I didn't know till last night, in fact. I forgot all about it until I heard them talking about it on Channel 3. That's when I pulled my ticket out and compared the numbers."

"And you didn't *call* us then?" Melissa said. "I can't believe it. I would've been burning up the phone wires."

"I wanted to make sure first," Kate admitted. "I mean, I had the ticket, but I wanted it official before I told anyone."

"You told Linda," Joanna said.

Kate had known this would be a bone of contention with Joanna who, for some reason, had always resented Kate's relationship with Linda. "I needed someone to come with me and figured she could get the day off more easily than anyone else." This was a thin excuse, and Kate knew it.

"Are you going to quit your job?" Melissa asked.

"I don't know. I haven't thought about it."

"I sure would," Melissa said.

"Mom," Tessa said, "does this mean I can go to the Rhode Island School of Design now?"

Kate grinned. "I guess it does, honey."

Tessa let out a whoop. RISD had been her dream ever since she'd decided she wanted to study interior design, but until now there was no way they could have afforded it.

"And I can go to Juilliard!" Nicole shouted.

Kate's family continued to fantasize about the lottery money until Kate finally managed to bring her children down to earth long enough to remind them that the world and their obligations—like homework and school—hadn't stopped with her lottery win.

"Oh, Kate, don't be such a wet blanket," Joanna said. "At least let them celebrate for *one* night."

Kate clenched her teeth and almost answered back with a sharp retort, but managed to stop herself in time. Joanna was just envious; Kate knew that. She sighed inwardly. Was it about to begin, then? Was Kate, even now, experiencing the first of the negative aspects of winning the lottery?

CHAPTER 3

"Well, what was the big family meeting about?"

Joanna Petro looked at her husband. "Where were you?" She'd called his office earlier to tell him about the meeting Kate had called, and he hadn't been in.

He shrugged. "I was having a drink with Rob."

Joanna studied him, trying to decide if Dave was telling her the truth.

"I must've just missed you," he said. "So what was it about?"

Joanna decided she preferred to believe him. "You'll never guess."

"Kate's getting married again?"

Joanna smiled. "That was my first idea, too. No, it's something much more exciting." She paused, stretching out the moment. "She's won the lottery."

It took him a few seconds for the news to sink in. When it did, his dark eyes widened. "Jesus. Are you *serious?*"

"Yes. Can you believe it?" Joanna was still having trouble believing it herself.

"How much did she win?"

"Twenty-eight million, after taxes."

He whistled. "So why the meeting? Is she giving everyone a share or something?"

Joanna had been wondering about that, too. "I don't know. She just said she wanted us all to know before the news is announced in tomorrow's paper."

Joanna couldn't help but think about how Kate had told Linda first. She frowned.

"What?" Dave said.

He always picked up on Joanna's feelings, even when she tried to hide them. It was one of the things that had attracted her to him initially, because in the beginning, if he sensed she was upset or unhappy, he had always tried to make her feel better by doing or saying something nice. Not so lately. But Joanna didn't want to think about that. Not now. Not until she'd figured out what to do about his disinterest. "Linda went with Kate to claim the money this morning," she said.

Normally, Dave would have dismissed her unvoiced resentment over Kate's relationship with Linda by saying something derogatory, but today he only gave a thoughtful nod. "You think she's gonna give Linda some of it?"

"Oh, I don't know, Dave." But Joanna had wondered about *that*, too.

"If she gives anyone money, it should be you, Mel and your mother."

Joanna agreed with him, but for some reason, she didn't want to say so. "I don't think she's had time to really think about it. She's still in shock."

"Well, if you're smart, you'll give her some hints. Hell, with twenty-eight million bucks, she can afford to give us a couple of million each. Maybe more." He grinned. "Think what we could do with a few million, babe."

Even though she told herself it was stupid to start counting her chickens before she knew for sure what Kate was planning, Joanna couldn't help herself. Because surely Kate *would* share.

Wouldn't she?

When Kate arrived at work on Tuesday morning, Darcy was already there. Seeing Kate, she said, "Oh, good. You're here. Is everything okay? I was worried." She peered at Kate closely.

Although, at fifty-two, she was only seven years older than Kate, Darcy was a motherly sort of woman who had always had a sympathetic interest in Kate. She'd once said she couldn't imagine how hard it was to be a divorced woman with four children.

Kate decided to tell Darcy what had happened now, even though she'd intended to wait until Dr. Holland had arrived so she could tell them both at the same time.

Darcy's brown eyes got bigger and bigger as Kate's revelation unfolded. "I just can't believe it," she said again and again.

"I know. I feel the same way," Kate said. "I keep thinking someone's going to say that it's all a joke."

"Oh, Kate, this is so wonderful." Darcy gave Kate a hug. "It couldn't happen to a more deserving person."

When Kate repeated her news to Dr. Holland half an hour later, he, too, seemed sincerely happy for her. "I know how you've struggled," he said, "and I've often wished I could afford to pay you more."

"Thank you," she said, touched by his kindness.

After that, the subject was dropped because the first patients began to arrive, and Kate was relieved. It hadn't even been twenty-four hours since she'd been authenticated as the official lottery winner, and she was already sick of the subject and especially sick of all the questions. But her relief was short-lived because by ten o'clock the morning paper had been read by most of the arriving patients, and everyone wanted to congratulate Kate and hear the whole story from her lips.

Short of being rude—something Kate couldn't bring herself to do—she tried to accommodate them as quickly and briefly as possible, reminding the more insistent ones that she had a job to do and needed to get back to it.

This continued unabated throughout the day. By twelve-fifteen, when the office closed for a forty-five-minute lunch break, Kate breathed a great sigh of relief. Maybe the worst part of today was over. But she soon discovered that it wasn't just the patients who wanted to see her and talk to her—there were also reporters camped outside. She had intended to go to the post office and pharmacy during the break—she'd packed a tuna sandwich and an apple so she didn't need to buy food—but when she saw the dozen or so people waiting for her to appear, she turned around and went back inside, ignoring their shouted questions.

"I can't believe this," she said to Darcy.

Darcy grimaced. "Bad, huh?"

"Look at them out there. They're like vultures."

"Maybe if you go out and talk to them for a few minutes, they'll go away," Darcy suggested.

"You think?"

"It's worth a try. Otherwise they may just hang out all day and get you tonight. After all, you can't hide out in here forever, and they know that."

Kate sighed. "Okay, I'll go out." Telling herself this was no big deal, she could do it, she headed out the front door once again.

Twenty minutes later, she felt battered by the barrage of questions, as well as frightened by the fact that not only were there reporters, there were also people she didn't know, people who wanted money from her.

One woman got belligerent when Kate, alarmed by her aggressiveness, said she wasn't doing anything with the money just now and that any requests would have to go through her attorney. She guessed a financial advisor wasn't the only person she needed to hire.

"You mean you won't help me, why don't you just admit it?" the woman shouted.

Kate shrank back from the hate in the woman's eyes. "I have to get back to work now," she said, turning to the reporters. "And I'd appreciate it if you would all leave."

The reporters did go, Darcy reported later (Kate was afraid to go out and check), but there were still people outside.

"Who *are* all these people?" Kate said, peering out the front window. "What makes them think they have a right to demand money from me?"

Darcy just shook her head. "Beats me. I could no more do something like that than chew tobacco." She smiled at Kate. "Cheer up, hon. This won't last forever. They'll get tired of stalking you when they see it doesn't do any good."

"You know, the pamphlet the lottery officials gave me warned of things like this. Part of me hoped they were exaggerating, but maybe they weren't."

As the afternoon wore on, several of the people wanting to tell Kate their sob stories came inside and asked to speak with her. Darcy firmly turned them away. The phone also rang incessantly. At four o'clock, it got so bad that Darcy called the police station, and two police officers came to the office and made the crowd disperse. But the officers didn't stay long, and it wasn't ten minutes after they had gone that several people showed up. Whether they were part of the original group or new hopefuls, Kate didn't know and didn't care. She just wanted them to go away and leave her alone.

By the end of the day, Kate was exhausted—not from work but from the stress of hiding and from the guilt over the disruption of the work day. She knew all the commotion had taken a toll on their normal efficiency. When Dr. Holland approached her as she got ready to leave and suggested it might be a good idea for her to take a leave of absence, "just till all this hubbub dies down," she gratefully accepted.

"Maybe," she said hesitantly, "I should just resign. Because you're going to need someone to do my job while I'm gone, anyway, and it'll probably be a lot easier to hire a permanent person than a temp."

"I hate losing you," he said. "You're one of the best employees I've ever had. But I think you're probably right."

Kate was a bit hurt that he so readily accepted her offer to leave, yet she understood his position. After all, he had a business to run—an important business—and sick people to serve. He didn't need chaos here, and her presence right now and for the foreseeable future might mean just that. There were tears in her eyes as she packed up her personal belongings and told Darcy goodbye.

"I'm going to miss you," Darcy said.

They hugged tightly, then Kate picked up her box of belongings and left the office by the back door. Luckily, no one was waiting in the back parking lot and by the time the people out front realized it was her driving off, it was too late for them to follow.

But again, Kate's relief didn't last long, for as she turned onto her street, she saw the crowd of people in front of her house.

"Oh, no." Her heart began to beat faster. The kids! Had any of these people tried to accost her kids? Why hadn't she thought about them today? She should have realized that if these people were smart enough to find out where she worked, it would be just as easy to find out where she lived.

Upset and worried, she pulled into her driveway and parked by the back gate. Before anyone could reach her, she was inside the gate and had securely locked it.

"Ms. Bishop! Ms. Bishop!" several voices called from the other side of the fence. A man peered over, but Kate ignored him. She ignored all of them except to say, "Go away and leave me alone!"

When she was inside, she made sure the door was locked, even though they never locked the back door when they were home. Cranbrook was a small town with little crime, and normally Kate and the kids felt very safe in their neighborhood. Not today. And maybe not ever again, she realized sadly.

"Mom!" Nicole said, coming into the kitchen. "Did you *see* the people outside? What do they want?"

"You didn't open the door and talk to them, did you?" Kate said.

"Of course not," Nicole said indignantly. "But what do they *want*?"

Kate sighed. "They want money."

"Money? From *us*?" Nicole said in disbelief. "But we don't know them."

"Obviously, as far as they're concerned, that's a minor detail."

Nicole seemed stunned.

"Where is everyone?" Kate asked, suddenly realizing how quiet it was in the house.

"Erin's at Heidi's. Her mom asked if she could go home with them, and I said sure. That was okay, wasn't it?"

Heidi Schuller was Erin's best friend. "Yes, that's fine. I'll call Mrs. Schuller later. What about Tessa?"

"She went to work. Tom took her. He said he'd be right back."

Kate chewed on her bottom lip. What if people started harassing Tessa at work? Walking over to the fridge where Tessa's and Tom's work schedules were posted, she saw that Tessa's shift had already begun. Picking up the phone, she called the café where Tessa was a combination hostess/cashier.

"Mom?" Tessa said when she recognized Kate's voice. "What's wrong?"

"I was just worried about you." Kate hurriedly told Tessa about all the people hanging around. "Be careful there. Don't talk to any strangers about the lottery."

"Don't worry, I won't."

"I mean it, Tessa. These people are nuts."

"I said I wouldn't, Mom. Quit worrying."

Kate sighed. "What time do you get off tonight?"

"Ten."

"I'll pick you up."

"You don't have to. Jenna's going to give me a ride."

"Okay, but don't get out of the car if you see anyone you don't recognize out front. If there's someone there, make Jenna pull into the back, okay?"

"Mom, don't be so paranoid. I'll be fine."

"You don't understand how crazy some of these people can be. A couple of them scared me today."

Tessa finally agreed, even though Kate knew her daughter thought she was exaggerating about the danger.

After that, the phone rang practically nonstop. In desperation, Kate finally took it off the hook. Unfortunately, she couldn't do that with the doorbell. When it rang for about the tenth time since she'd gotten home from work, Kate was ready to scream. If this was another of those damned reporters, she would call the police.

Kate walked out to the entryway and called out, "Who is it?"

"It's me, Mark."

Breathing a sigh of relief, Kate opened the door to her ex-husband.

"Dammit, Kate, why aren't you answering the phone? I've been trying to call you for hours."

"Because the phone hasn't stopped ringing since I

got home. I couldn't take it anymore. Practically everyone I've ever known has called. I'm sorry," she added, seeing his face.

"Well, you should be," he said angrily. "What if it was an emergency? What about the kids? What if I needed to talk to one of them?"

She couldn't help it; she smiled. "You do know where we live."

Instead of answering her statement, he said, "Why didn't you call me? Why did I have to hear about what happened from someone else?"

Kate sighed. "I'm sorry," she said again. "I didn't think to call you."

"Didn't *think*? Jesus, Kate, I should have been the *first* person you called."

Involuntarily, she stiffened. "And why is that?"

"Because I'm the kids' father, for Christ's sake. This affects me as much as it affects them, don't you think?"

"How do you figure that?"

He stared at her. Before he could answer, Erin—who had arrived home half an hour earlier—came racing down the hall. "Dad! Did you hear? We're rich!" She threw her arms around him in an exuberant hug.

"Yeah, I heard." His blue eyes met Kate's over Erin's head.

"We can do anything we want!" Erin said. Breaking the hug, she grinned up at Kate. "Mom's gonna buy me a horse."

Kate raised her eyebrows. "Oh?" There had been no discussion of horses or anything else last night, at least not on her part. "And where would we keep a horse?"

Erin frowned. Her glasses had slid down her nose when she'd hugged her father, and she pushed them back up. "Aren't we gonna buy a new house? Nicole said we probably w—"

"Erin," Kate interrupted. "Your dad and I would like to talk privately, okay?" Turning to Mark, she added, "Come on out to the kitchen. I've got some Dos Equis in the fridge." She wondered what a shrink would think about the fact she always kept his favorite beer on hand.

"Let me just go say hi to the others first," he said. "Are they in their rooms?"

"Tom's out with friends," Kate said. "And Tessa insisted on going to work, even though I didn't want her to. But Nicole's here."

A few minutes later, Mark joined her in the kitchen. After getting himself a beer, he sat at the table.

Kate had already fixed herself a cup of her favorite raspberry tea. "Look," she said, "you're right, I *should* have called you. I just didn't think. Truth is, I was so stunned yesterday, I could hardly think about anything. My mind kept going around in circles." She sipped some of her tea and smiled at him. "It's incredible, isn't it?"

For the first time since arriving, he seemed to relax.

His answering smile was warm. "I couldn't believe it when I heard." He shook his head. "Twenty-eight million bucks. It's mind-boggling."

"I still haven't really taken it in. I mean, I know it's a tremendous amount of money, but right now it doesn't seem real. It's just words." Then she thought about the reporters who had been camped outside her office today. And the others who had congregated outside the house. "Although it's beginning to seem *more* real," she added dryly.

"It's going to change everyone's life," he said.

For the second time since he'd shown up on the doorstep, something about what he'd said and the way he'd said it hit Kate the wrong way. Had he forgotten that although he was the children's father, he was no longer her husband? Even though she felt like saying so, all she did was nod. "Yes, it will," she said. "But I'm determined not to do anything too quickly. It would be easy to go crazy and start buying things—like that horse Erin is obviously fantasizing about—but I'm not going to." She told him about the pamphlet the lottery officials had given her, about the horror stories it had listed. "I have no intention of ending up like those people."

"I agree," he said. "You need to make smart investments and protect that money. What you keep, that is."

"Yes, well, I haven't thought that far ahead yet. Right now the money is safely deposited in the bank, and that's where it's going to stay until I consult a financial advisor and a lawyer."

"What do you need a lawyer for? Hell, you don't even need a financial advisor. I can help you with all that. In fact, I'd be glad to."

Kate must have looked as aghast as she felt. Mark advise her about money? That was a joke. When they'd been married, she'd been the one to handle finances. Left to him, they'd have been lucky to be able to buy a house. He had the poorest judgment when it came to money of anyone she knew. Well, aside from Joanna's husband, she amended wryly. Money ran through Dave's fingers like water.

"I've been studying the markets," Mark said in answer to her unspoken criticism.

Kate refrained from rolling her eyes. She wanted to say he struggled to pay his bills. Where had he thought he'd get the money to play the market? Yet his unrealistic attitude didn't surprise her.

Mark had always been a dreamer. Someone who moved from one job or project or idea to another. Someone who never finished anything he started. Someone who always thought the grass was greener somewhere else. This trait had made her crazy when they were married. Thank God he was no longer her responsibility. He had a new wife. Let *her* worry about him.

"I think it would be wise for me to use someone entirely impartial, someone with lots of experience," she said.

"You don't trust me, do you? Jesus, Kate. Of all the people in the world, you know I have the kids' best interest, *your* best interest, at heart."

"I'm sure you do. But I still think a professional financial advisor is the way to go."

He seemed about to say something else, but after a moment simply shrugged. "It's your money. I guess you can do what you want."

Yes, she thought, *it is, and I can.* "I appreciate the offer, though." She finished her tea and glanced at the clock. It was ten o'clock. Tessa would be home soon. "Listen, I'm exhausted. I need to get to sleep. Let's plan to talk again on the weekend, okay? By then I'll have a better idea of things. But one thing I want you to know before you go is, you no longer have to worry about child support. I know that'll ease things for you and Hillary."

She almost added that she'd also buy him a new truck or SUV—his pickup had seen lots better days and she knew he couldn't afford a new one—but she bit back the offer. She really *did* need to think things through carefully before she started making promises to people.

Guiltily, she thought about how she'd promised Linda a new car and freedom from her credit card debt. Not to mention buying the building Linda leased. But as quickly as the guilt had formed, Kate banished it. Of all the people in the world, Linda had been there for her most consistently. She'd comforted her in the bad times and celebrated with her in the good times. Kate loved her, and if she wanted to do nice things for her now, that was her business and no one else's. Certainly it had nothing to do with Mark.

Later, after she was in bed and the house was quiet, Kate thought about everything Mark had said and everything he hadn't said. When she'd told him about not having to pay child support anymore, she could tell the news wasn't the nice surprise she'd expected it to be. Naively expected it to be, she realized.

He wants more. He probably expected me to say I was going to give him a big chunk of the money. Maybe a couple of million. This realization astounded her. It had never crossed her mind to give him any of her winnings. Why should it? He wasn't her husband. If their situations were reversed, she doubted he'd give *her* anything. Well, maybe that wasn't true. Maybe he would. After all, their children lived with her.

Kate sighed. Oh, hell. Maybe she *would* give him something. She certainly had enough to do so. But even as she thought it, she had a feeling that no matter what she gave him, it probably would be less than he expected.

CHAPTER 4

Kate was almost afraid to look outside on Wednesday morning when she awoke. Warily, she peeked between the slats of the blinds in the dining room and felt weak with relief when she saw there wasn't anyone out front. After yesterday, she hadn't known what to expect. She did know that the first thing she intended to do today was get an unlisted phone number. Next, she intended to purchase cell phones for all the kids as well as a new one for herself and possibly hire a security service to patrol outside the house—at least until things settled down.

While she waited for her coffee to brew, she made lists. Find a lawyer. Find a financial advisor. Call her mother first, though, because maybe she'd have some recommendations. Besides, knowing her mother, she'd be irritated if Kate *didn't* ask for her advice.

Kate sighed. She sighed a lot when she thought about her mother. If only she had the kind of mother whose feelings would be hurt if Kate didn't seek her opinion. That, Kate could understand.

But no, not Harriet August. She wasn't the hurt-feelings type. Disapproval was more her speed. Her attitude was, if you were stupid enough not to realize she knew best, you deserved what you got. And the most frustrating part of Kate's relationship with her mother was that her mother usually *was* right. And naturally she never hesitated to say, "I told you so."

Kate poured herself a mug of coffee, added a generous amount of powdered creamer and a heaping teaspoon of Splenda, then stood at the kitchen window, which faced east, and watched the sun come up as she sipped.

Harriet August hadn't had an easy life. The oldest of five children in a blue-collar family, with a father whose livelihood was precarious at best, she had worked her way through college and become an elementary school teacher, a position she'd held for more than forty years. Kate's father had been a teacher, too. Unfortunately, he'd died in a freak accident when they had only been married fifteen years. They were both thirty-seven years old. Joanna had been fourteen, Kate twelve and Melissa, the youngest, barely a year old.

The insurance paid off their home, with a bit left over, but it was still a struggle to raise her daughters. "A thankless task," she'd once said during a particularly bitter conversation with Kate where she was bemoaning the fact that none of her daughters had ever finished college. Both Joanna and Kate had dropped out to get married. Melissa had refused to go altogether, saying she'd had enough of school.

"How your father and I, who both valued education so much, could have three children who don't value it at all, is beyond me," Harriet had cried.

Kate felt her accusation was unfair and had said so. "You know I wish I'd been able to get my degree," she'd said, "but it was more important to get Mark through school."

"If you hadn't insisted on getting married at twenty, you *would* have finished," her mother retorted. "At least, though, you were sensible enough not to start having children until Mark had his degree."

Faint praise was better than no praise at all, Kate had decided.

But Harriet's frustration with her daughters wasn't limited to their perceived lack of appreciation for higher education or the sacrifices she'd made to save for something they didn't care about; she simply couldn't understand why they wouldn't listen to her when she gave them advice. Never mind the advice hadn't been asked for and wasn't wanted. They were her daughters; it was her responsibility to give them the benefit of her experience and wisdom.

Kate did understand this, more so now that her children were growing up and developing their own ideas, which were often at cross-purposes with hers. But she still felt that at some point in your children's lives, you owed them the privilege of allowing them to make their own mistakes. And it *was* a privilege. How else were children to learn? Learning from your mistakes was the path to maturity and wisdom.

Sighing again, Kate finished her coffee and poured herself a second cup. It was time to wake the kids, time to stop brooding over her mother and their differences. Her mother would never change. Kate simply had to accept her as she was.

For the next hour, she didn't have time to think about much except getting everyone off to work or school. She insisted on driving Nicole and Erin, even though Erin enjoyed meeting Heidi and walking with her.

"But *why* can't I walk?" she whined.

"You know why, Erin. Remember all those people outside last night? They scared me. I'm afraid…" She hesitated. Did she really want Erin to know she was worried about some nut kidnapping her? "I don't want anyone following you," she said firmly.

"We'll ride bikes, then."

"I don't want you riding your bike, either."

"You mean I can't ever ride my bike *again?*"

Kate didn't know what to say. "I didn't say you couldn't ever ride your bike again, honey. I just…for now, I want to make sure none of those people bother you."

Erin frowned. With her tendency to worry about everything, plus her innate intelligence, she had clearly picked up on what Kate hadn't said.

Tessa was getting a ride to school with a friend, so Kate didn't have to worry about her.

Cars, Kate thought as she drove the younger girls to their respective schools. She would put new cars for both Tessa and Tom on her list of things to do this week. Then she would no longer have to worry about Tom driving that old clunker of his—the only thing he'd been able to afford when he'd started his job last year—and Tessa would finally be independent and not have to rely on him or Kate or her friends.

So she would be buying four cars to start with. One for herself, one for Linda and one each for Tom and Tessa. Oh, hell, she might as well just order a dozen. Why not give her mother and sisters new cars, too? And why leave Mark out? He might no longer be her husband, but, as he'd pointed out, he *was* the kids' father. She could afford to give all her nieces and nephews new cars, as well. Not that there were that many of them: Joanna had two sons and a daughter, and Melissa had just the one daughter.

Shoot, Kate thought happily, as she got back to the house, buying a dozen new cars wouldn't even put a dent in her winnings. For the first time, she began to realize just how much she'd really won. Thinking about a dozen new cars and how little of the money it would take to pay for them had put the whole thing into perspective for her.

Yes, there was a price to pay for winning all that

money. She'd lost her privacy—at least for now—but hopefully all this hubbub would die down and people would lose interest in her once they realized she wasn't going to hand out money to anyone who asked.

And if it didn't? If people continued to pester her and show up at the house?

Well, she guessed she'd just have to move then.

Feeling better now, she began to look forward to her day.

Kate had just finished talking to a representative at the telephone company about a new, unlisted phone number when the doorbell rang. She almost forgot to call out, "Yes? Who is it?" instead of just opening the door as she had in the past.

"Ms. Bishop? My name is Luke Ruskin and I wanted to talk to you about a terrific opportunity you won't want to pass up."

Oh, for crying out loud. What was *with* these people? "Go away, Mr. Ruskin. I'm not interested in anything you have to say."

"Just give me ten minutes of your time. Just ten minutes. I promise you, you won't be sorry."

Just then, Ginger, roused from her bed in a corner of the kitchen, began to bark.

Kate walked away from the door. Let the man talk all he wanted; she wasn't letting him in. But she quickly decided she couldn't just ignore him, because he started to bang on the door in between calling out to her. He obviously wasn't going to go away. And the more he banged, the louder Ginger barked.

Kate walked back to the foyer and called out again. "Mr. Ruskin? If you don't go away immediately, I'm letting the dog out, and believe me, you don't want that." Ginger *sounded* ferocious, even though, to Kate's knowledge, she'd never bitten anyone in her life.

Apparently he realized from Kate's tone that she meant business because he quit pounding on the door and a few seconds later, she heard his footsteps hurrying away.

"Now settle down, Ginger," Kate said, rubbing the dog's head in thanks. "He's going."

Walking into the dining room, she peered out the front window and saw him getting into a dark SUV which was parked out front. She was about to go back to the kitchen to make more phone calls when she saw another car—this one a blue sedan—park across the street. A stocky man in a dark-blue suit got out and began walking toward the house.

She recognized Ward McAndrews, the president of the bank. "Damn," she said softly, looking down at herself.

She hadn't had a shower yet. Had just thrown on faded jeans and a dark-green sweater and shoved her sockless feet into old clogs. She *had* combed her hair and put on some lipstick, but that was all. She certainly wasn't dressed the way she'd planned to be when she talked to Ward. For the two minutes it took him to reach the front door and ring the doorbell, she actually considered pretending she wasn't home. But she quickly realized how childish that behavior would be.

Who cared how she looked? She was in the driver's seat here. She was the one whose business Ward McAndrews would be cultivating, for she was certain that's exactly why he was calling at—she looked at her watch—9:14 in the morning. The only surprise was that the money had already reached the bank.

But maybe it hadn't, she realized as she walked to the door. Maybe he was just hoping to make sure she *did* deposit it with him.

"Hello, Ward," she said with a smile as she opened the door. "Come in." Ginger had begun to bark again, but Kate held on to her collar to let her know Ward was okay and to keep her from jumping on him, a bad habit that Kate had been unable to break.

"Hello, Kate," he said heartily, even as he cast a wary glance at the dog, who was straining against her firm hold. His face was red, probably from the exertion of his walk from car to door. Ward was quite obviously overweight and out of shape. "My, my, you must be floating today. Such a lucky girl."

"Hush, Ginger. I have to admit, it's pretty exciting." She beckoned him to follow her back to the family room, then belatedly remembered the hole in the ceiling. Oh, well. Who cared about that, either? In fact, she thought in amusement, right now she didn't much care about anything except keeping the leeches away. She bit back a grin. Maybe Ward McAndrews was one of them. She guessed she would soon see.

She saw him glance up at the blue oilcloth tacked to the ceiling and, it was obvious from his expression, think about whether he should mention it or pretend it wasn't there.

Kate grinned. "We had a leak in the roof and it caused water to build up in the attic." The grin morphed into a chuckle. "I discovered the caved-in ceiling Saturday morning. But Saturday night I won the lottery. So that solved *that* problem. We're getting a new roof put on later this week." She indicated the battered leather sofa. "Have a seat. I'll put the dog out back. Otherwise she'll be all over you."

Once the dog was safely removed, Kate walked back into the den. "Would you like some coffee?"

"No, thank you, Kate. I just dropped in to say how pleased I am that you have chosen our bank to be the guardian of your money."

"So it's already arrived?"

"Not yet. I did get a call from lottery officials notifying me that it would be coming today."

"Good. I'm glad to see they're on the ball."

"Now I know someone as smart as you won't want to just let the money sit in your checking account."

Kate bit back a smile. This was the first time Ward

had ever referred to her as smart. In fact, even though his wife, Sharon, and Kate's mother played bridge together and were fairly good friends, Ward had mostly ignored Kate. She'd been small potatoes, not worth his time. "No, of course not," she said. "That really *would* be stupid, wouldn't it?"

"I'm glad you agree. Of course, I knew you would. So I wanted to assure you that we have many wonderful investment options for you. I thought I'd draw up an investment plan and then we can sit down together later this week and go over it and you can choose what suits you best." He smiled happily. "How does that sound?"

Kate was having a hard time keeping a serious expression in the face of his obsequiousness. She almost said, *Oh, please, you don't really think I'm going to allow a small-town banker whose financial knowledge is probably not much more sophisticated than mine to handle twenty-eight million dollars.*

But good manners and good sense—she had to live in Cranbrook, she didn't want to make enemies—prevailed. "Gosh, Ward, I'm not sure a week is long enough to think about how I might want to invest the money. However, if you want to make a list of what the bank can offer, that would be great. I'm planning to talk with a professional financial advisor this week and I'll be happy to give him the list."

Ward frowned. "Now, Katie, you don't need to bring

in an outsider. Why, *I'm* a professional financial advisor myself and, as a good friend of your mother's, I feel an obligation to make sure no one takes advantage of you."

"And I appreciate that, Ward. It's very thoughtful of you."

"Sometimes it's difficult to know the difference between a legitimate advisor and a charlatan."

"I'm sure it can be."

He looked uncertain, and she knew he was wondering how far he could push.

Kate stood. "I really appreciate your coming by."

Because he had no choice, he stood, too. She knew he wanted to continue trying to persuade her to let him take charge of her winnings and was trying to think of a convincing argument.

"I'm sorry, Ward, but I've got an appointment in—" she looked at her watch "—an hour and a half, so I'd better start getting ready." She began to walk toward the foyer. "I'll drop by the bank on Friday to pick up that list, okay?"

"All right," he said, reluctantly following her once more.

When they reached the front door, she opened it, smiled and said, "Goodbye, Ward."

He hesitated. "Just promise me one thing, Katie. Don't make any decisions without consulting me first, okay? Some of these so-called advisors are only out for what they can get from you."

As if you aren't....

"I'll definitely keep that in mind," she said sweetly. She shut the door firmly behind him.

"Mom?"

"Hello, Kate. I wondered if I'd hear from you today."

Why did Harriet *always* have to sound slightly critical? Trying not to sound defensive, Kate said, "I meant to call earlier, but Ward McAndrews came to see me and he just left. Before I forget, I wanted to give you our new phone number. It's unlisted."

"New *phone* number? Why?"

Kate explained what had been happening.

"What a world we live in," her mother said when she'd finished. "I can't believe people were camped outside your house. That's really frightening."

"Yes, it is. Not so much for me. Mostly the people here yesterday just wanted to ask me for money and I don't think they were dangerous. But there *are* nuts out there and I am worried about the kids."

"Maybe you should think about moving to a secure neighborhood. One of those gated communities that are springing up all over the place."

"I hope it doesn't come to that, but I'll move if I have to. In the meantime, I'm going to hire a security service."

"A security service! Is that *really* necessary?"

"Maybe not, but it'll make me feel better."

"Why can't you just call Scott Logan?"

Scott Logan was Cranbrook's new chief of police. He'd been a high school classmate of Kate's, and she liked him. "Mom, the Cranbrook police force has a grand total of six officers to cover three shifts every single day. I don't think they'd be able to spare anyone to watch the house."

"What do we pay them for, anyway?" her mother grumbled.

"I'd rather have a private service. That way, if I'm not happy with them, I can fire them."

"That's true," her mother conceded. "You're right. That's probably the way to go."

Kate nearly dropped the phone, she was so astounded. Her mother was *agreeing* with her? With no argument to speak of? Was the sky falling? Had hell frozen over?

"What did Ward McAndrews want?" her mother was now saying.

She listened quietly as Kate told her about the visit.

"That was wise," she said when Kate finished. "Ward may *think* he knows a lot, but the biggest account he's ever handled is Hollister's, and they don't keep *all* their assets in his bank. I know, because Gerri told me so." Gerri Hollister and her brother Blaine were the co-owners of a highly successful chain of convenience stores.

Hell *must* have frozen over. That was two you're-rights in one day.

"Who would you suggest I ask for a recommendation on a financial advisor?" Kate said when her shock had worn off.

"Let me give Gerri a call. She'll know someone, I'm sure."

"Okay, great. And while you're at it, ask her if she knows a good attorney."

"*I* know a good attorney, Kate. Adam Marino."

Kate should have thought of Adam Marino herself. The son of the mayor of Cranbrook, he had graduated from Cornell Law School at the top of his class, refused all the highly paid job offers with big law firms that had been offered to him, and instead come back to Cranbrook to set up a private practice.

Adam Marino was considered brilliant. He was also drop-dead handsome and the most eligible and sought-after bachelor in town. Kate's heart skipped just *thinking* about having a reason to call Adam Marino, even though he was nine years younger than she was and totally out of her league.

"You're right," she said. "I'll call him this afternoon."

"Call him now," her mother said. "While I call Gerri."

Kate couldn't help grinning. Her mother was back to normal. All was right with the world.

CHAPTER 5

Kate had just reached for the phone book to look up Adam Marino's number when the doorbell rang again. She moaned. Now what? Maybe this time she really *would* pretend not to be home. Yet even as she thought this, her curiosity got the better of her and she couldn't resist peeking out the dining room window to see if she could get a glimpse of whoever the visitor was. As soon as she spied the ten-year-old silver Honda Accord in her driveway, she realized it was her sister Melissa at the door.

"Coming," she called.

"Hey!" Melissa said, reaching out to give Kate a hug. "I tried to call you at work, but they said you'd quit. Then when I tried you here, I got a recording saying your number was disconnected. What's up?"

As always, Kate's youngest sister looked gorgeous, even though she, like Kate, wore faded jeans she'd paired with a gray sweatshirt. With her green eyes, blond hair, perfect complexion and slender yet curvy body, Melissa was the beauty in the family—had even won a couple of beauty contests in her teens.

"I arranged for an unlisted number this morning," Kate said as they walked into the kitchen. "Want some coffee?"

"Dying for some."

After pouring them each a mug, Kate joined Melissa at the kitchen table.

"See? I *knew* you'd quit your job," Melissa said, stirring Splenda into her coffee.

"It wasn't my choice." Kate went on to explain what had happened the day before. "I'll miss working there."

"Oh, come on, Kate, why would you want to stay there, anyway? I mean, you can do anything you want to do. Believe me, if *I'd* won, I'd be traveling all over the world." She grinned. "Hey, I'm available anytime you want to go somewhere. Think about it. We could have a blast together."

"What about *your* job?" Kate asked. Melissa was a waitress at an upscale restaurant in the neighboring town of Hudson and actually seemed to be enjoying this job, which hadn't been the case with her last couple. She tended to change positions often. She was a female Mark, always thinking the grass was greener somewhere else. Her lack of drive frustrated Kate, because of all of them, Melissa had the most natural talent. She could have done so many things in life, yet she'd spent most of her energy on here-today-gone-tomorrow men.

"There are always other restaurants," Melissa said with a dismissive shrug.

"You know, Mel, it might be a good idea—"

"Don't say it, Kate. I get enough lectures from Mom."

"I know. Sorry."

"Thing is, when you're a waitress, it doesn't matter if you change jobs a lot. If you're good, you can always find another one...usually a better one, too."

Kate nodded, even though she didn't agree with Melissa.

Melissa grinned. "So where are we going to go first?"

Kate tried to decide if her sister was kidding or serious. "I'm not sure I'm going anywhere. I have to think things through before I do anything."

"Kate, you're so damned *serious*. What's to think about? Can't you just have some fun for a change? Don't you realize that with all that money you no longer have to worry about *anything*?"

"I've got four kids. I can't just take off and *have fun*, as you put it."

"Sure you can. Tom and Tessa are old enough to be on their own. I'm sure they're dying to, anyway. *We* certainly were when *we* were their age. You said yourself that now you can afford it, Tessa can go off to that school in Rhode Island. So that only leaves Erin and Nicole, and I'm sure Mom would be happy to come and stay with them. You know how she likes to run things."

"What about Leeann?" Leeann was Melissa's fifteen-year-old daughter.

Melissa's expression hardened. "I'm thinking of sending her off to a boarding school."

Kate blinked. "Boarding school?"

"I can't deal with her anymore. She won't listen to me."

Kate almost asked how Melissa expected to pay for a boarding school, but she was afraid she knew the answer. Mel probably expected *her* to pay. "What's the problem now?" Better to ignore the subject of boarding school.

Melissa drained her coffee and looked at the pot. "Mind if I finish that off?"

"Help yourself."

"Well, besides the fact her grades are in the toilet, that she ignores any curfew I set, and that she has a mouth on her that won't quit," Melissa said as she got up and walked to the counter, "now she's in love. She's met some guy…he's older…she won't tell me *how* old, of course…but I suspect he's nineteen or twenty. They're having sex, of course. She practically flung *that* piece of information at me. I ought to have that guy arrested. After all, she's a minor."

"Oh, dear," Kate said. She refrained from mentioning that Melissa had been having sex since she was sixteen, because of course, they both knew that.

"When I told her what she was doing was stupid, she said she *wasn't* stupid—that she'd gotten a prescription for birth control pills."

Kate couldn't help thinking about Nicole. What would she do if she found out Nicole was sexually active?

"I guess I'm glad she had sense enough to get them," Mel continued, "because I sure as hell don't want her getting pregnant like I did. Even though *I* was seventeen when it happened." She sat down at the table again. "I don't know, Kate. I guess I just figured if I sent her away, she'd be forced to straighten up."

"Mel, look, I'm not trying to tell you what to do, but I don't think sending Leeann away is the answer. As stubborn and rebellious as she is right now, she'd probably run away. After all, as soon as she's sixteen she's no longer considered a minor and she can drop out of school legally. At least, I think she can. I'd have to look that up."

"Well, what do you suggest? I'm at my wit's end with her."

You could try setting her a better example. Kate felt guilty over the thought, because she really did love Mel, but the truth was, Mel wasn't exactly an exemplary mother. She ran through boyfriends like a hot knife through butter. And, unfortunately, many of those men slept over, and Leeann knew it. What was the kid *supposed* to think when her mother acted as if it was no big deal to have sex with anyone she fancied? But how could Kate say those things? She'd tried, several times, to gently suggest Mel might want to be more discreet, but Mel had shrugged off her comments, saying Kate was old-fashioned and had no idea what it was like nowadays.

"Men *expect* sex," she'd said. "It's part of the deal. They pay for the night on the town and you give them sex in return."

Kate hadn't agreed with that, either, but it was true that she was totally out of touch when it came to the dating game. She'd married young, and since her divorce she'd been too busy working and raising her kids to have either the time or the energy to date.

"I'm no expert," Kate finally said. "Raising kids isn't easy and most of us just muddle along hoping we're doing something right. But I do think you should try talking to her, not in an accusatory way, just as her mom who loves her and wants the best for her."

Melissa shrugged. "Maybe. We'll see." Then she brightened. "But let's not talk about Leeann anymore. Let's talk about the money. That's a heckuva lot more fun. C'mon. Let's plan a trip. I've always wanted to go to London and Paris. And I know Joanna would go in a heartbeat."

"I can't plan a trip," Kate said, although she had to admit she was tempted. It *would* be fun to take her sisters somewhere. The three of them hadn't had a vacation together since they were kids. "I have to call Adam Marino."

"Adam Marino!"

Kate grinned at the expression on Mel's face. "I need a lawyer and Mom suggested him."

"Oh, you lucky dog. I wish *I* had a reason to call him.

He's so hot, he sizzles. But why does calling him mean you can't plan a trip?"

"I just meant I can't think about going anywhere till I get things in order. I need a new will, for starters. And there are other things that need to be done. The roofers are coming on Friday to begin work on the house. And I need to go look at cars." Now it was her turn to grin. "I'm buying everyone a new car, including you and Joanna and Mom."

"Really?" Mel squealed. She jumped up and came around the table to hug Kate. "Oh, I've always wanted a bright red Corvette convertible." Her eyes shone.

"I, um, was thinking more along the lines of new Toyota or Honda sedans."

"Sedans!"

Kate took one look at the disappointment on her sister's face and sighed. "Oh, okay. You can have a convertible. But let's make it something a bit more sensible than a Corvette."

"BMW?" Mel said hopefully.

Kate rolled her eyes. "We'll see."

This earned Kate another exuberant hug. "You're the best," Mel said, picking up her shoulder bag and preparing to leave.

"Write down my new phone number before you go," Kate said, motioning to the spiral notebook lying on the counter next to the phone.

After her sister left, Kate rinsed out the coffeepot,

wiped off the table and put the two mugs in the dish-washer. Then she once more reached for the phone book. This time she didn't intend to let anything distract her from making the call to Adam Marino's office.

Melissa belted out "Desecration Smile" along with the Red Hot Chili Peppers as she drove to work an hour later. For about the millionth time, she wished she had a top-of-the-line CD player in her car, but she hadn't been able to afford one.

If I'd won the lottery instead of Kate…

Lost in a daydream of how she'd spend all those millions, she barreled right through the Stop sign at First and Main streets, narrowly missing hitting a battered white pickup truck, whose male driver yelled something at her, then gave her the finger.

"Oh, up yours," she muttered. Jolted out of her pleasant thoughts, her mind turned to her daughter. Leeann had skipped school today. There'd been a message from the high school attendance clerk when Mel had gotten home after visiting Kate. Leeann was probably with that boyfriend of hers again. *What the hell am I going to do with her? She's out of control.* Melissa heaved a long-suffering sigh. Geez. If only girls knew what their sweet little babies were going to grow up to be and how many headaches they'd give their mothers, no one would *ever* get pregnant.

Melissa remembered how Harriet had wanted her to

go off somewhere to have her baby, then give it up for adoption. She remembered how she'd fought her mother, saying she'd *never* give her baby up, *never*. Now, she thought ruefully, there were many days when she wondered why she'd been so determined to keep Leeann. If she'd had any *idea* what was in store for her…

Oh, hell, who was she kidding? At that stage of her life, if Harriet had said it was sunny outside, Melissa would have insisted it wasn't, all evidence to the contrary. She'd *lived* to disagree with her mother. Was *proud* of the fact that she wasn't like her mother.

We all were. All three of us defied her.

Yet they all loved their mother, Mel knew. It was just that Harriet was so damned sure she was right about everything. It made Mel crazy. *And it makes me do stupid things just to piss her off….*

The realization was sobering.

Is that what was happening with Leeann now? Was she purposely doing things to make Mel mad?

Melissa was still thinking about her daughter as she pulled into the employee parking lot behind Slater's Dockside, the restaurant where she'd worked the past five months. It was located on Hudson Lake, named for the Hudson family, who had once owned all the property in this area. Slater's was renowned for its steaks and baby back ribs, as well as the best double-fudge brownies to be found anywhere.

As Mel walked into the restaurant, Connie Slater looked at the clock. "You're late."

Mel frowned. It was only 11:10. Why was Connie worked up about ten minutes? "Sorry. Traffic was heavy this morning."

"You should leave earlier, Mel."

Mel bit back the sarcastic remark she wanted to make. Obviously Connie was out of sorts today. "Where is everyone?"

"We called a meeting. They're all in the party room. You're the last to arrive." Beckoning Mel to follow, Connie strode off.

What was up? Mel wondered.

She didn't have long to wonder, for she'd no sooner sat down with the other waitstaff and kitchen staff than Whit Slater, Connie's husband, said, "Connie and I just wanted you all to know before it becomes public knowledge that we have decided to put Slater's up for sale."

Gasps followed this announcement. Mel was shocked. Slater's was a rip-roaring success, the kind of place that the owners usually decided to duplicate in other locations. She couldn't imagine why they were selling.

That question, too, was quickly answered.

"This isn't the kind of thing I want everyone to know," Whit continued. "We plan to say we're ready to retire and have some time to enjoy life. But the truth is…" Here he paused and seemed to struggle before continuing. "I've been diagnosed with lung cancer and

will be undergoing treatment in Houston at M.D.
Anderson." He reached for Connie's hand. She gave
him a tremulous smile. "No matter the outcome of my
treatment, we need to concentrate on our health and
our family. Much as we hate it, Slater's has to go."

Mel's heart went out to them. Connie could be a pill
sometimes—she was a demanding perfectionist—but
she was also generous and good-hearted. Mel knew for
a fact that Connie and Whit had helped employees
who were having a rough time. And they loved Slater's.
They'd put heart and soul into it for years. It was too
bad they didn't have a kid interested in taking it over,
but their only child, a daughter named Annette, was
married to a career Navy pilot and currently they were
living in Japan.

Whit continued to talk about what was going to
happen in the next weeks. "We hope to sell quickly.
Slater's is a great opportunity for someone who knows
the restaurant business. In fact, if *you* know anyone who
might be interested, tell them to call Bucky Spencer.
He'll be handling everything for us." Looking at
Connie again, he said, "Connie and I are leaving for
Houston on Sunday."

"Who'll be in charge while you're gone?" The
question came from James Colbert, the head chef.

"My sister Evvie," Connie said.

"And George Pinkus said he'd fill in as long as
needed," Whit added.

George Pinkus was one of Whit's closest friends and his first employer; he'd been retired for a number of years now but occasionally helped out when Slater's was swamped.

Long after the meeting was over, Mel was still thinking about how unpredictable life could be. Everything was fine one minute and the next, everything was changed. She felt sorry for the Slaters; they didn't deserve this. But who *did* deserve cancer? It was a horrible disease, striking people right and left. In fact, it seemed to Mel as if more and more people were getting cancer than ever before. Just last month the sister of a good friend of hers had died of colon cancer. She'd been just thirty-six.

Mel was also thinking about the fate of Slater's. And suddenly, about three o'clock, the wildest idea popped into her mind. At first, she almost dismissed it, but the more she thought about it, the more excited she became. Maybe her idea wasn't so wild, after all.

Hell, *she* knew the restaurant business. Hadn't she worked in it for years? Mostly as a waitress, of course, but so what?

This was the opportunity of a lifetime. Her chance at the brass ring. She almost called Kate on her break to sound her out about financing the venture, but something stopped her. Maybe it would be a better idea to call Bucky Spencer in the morning, get all the facts and figures. Have her ducks in a row before she approached Kate.

Mel smiled. Yes, that was the way to go. If she presented her case in a businesslike manner, Kate couldn't refuse. After all, she had more money than she could ever spend, even if she lived ten lifetimes.

CHAPTER 6

"Hey, pigster!"

Recognizing Joshua Melton's taunting voice, Erin gritted her teeth. "Shut up, Joshua," she muttered under her breath and refused to turn around.

"Wait up, four eyes."

I hate him. I hate him. She began to walk faster, hoping to get to the science lab before he caught up with her. Unfortunately, her progress was blocked by a group of kids congregating in front of the library, and she had to wend her way around them. By the time she was on the other side, Joshua was right behind her.

"So you're too good to talk to me now, huh?" he said. Recently he'd lost one of his last baby teeth and his grin revealed the gap.

Erin stuck her chin up and made her voice as withering as she could manage. "I have no idea what you're talking about." She hated the way her heart was beating too fast.

In answer, Joshua yanked on her ponytail. "Why did you stop wearing your hair in *pigtails?*"

Because you started calling me a pigster, you moron, that's why. Although Erin knew ignoring him was her best option, she couldn't seem to stop herself from saying, "None of your business."

His smile infuriated her because it seemed to say he knew what she was thinking and feeling. Oh, God. She would die if he really did know how she felt. Because the thought frightened her so badly, she quickly added, "Why don't you go bother someone who *cares* what you think?"

For a couple of seconds, he didn't say anything, just looked into her eyes over the rims of her glasses— which, of course, had once again slid down her nose. Then, in a moment she knew she'd relive over and over again for the rest of the day and probably all night, too, he leaned forward and whispered, "When you wear those pigtails, it makes me want to kiss you. Maybe even ask you to the eighth-grade dance."

She could hardly concentrate in science class. She kept hearing Joshua's voice, and each time she did, her stomach got that hollow feeling again, and her heart felt like it was going to end up in her throat.

"What's *wrong* with you today?" asked Cindy Pinchuck, her lab partner. "That's the second time you handed me the wrong thing."

"Sorry," Erin said, swallowing.

Stop thinking about him! But she couldn't, because no matter how many times she told herself she couldn't stand Joshua Melton, didn't care *at all* what he thought, wouldn't go to the eighth-grade dance with him if he *begged*, she knew she was lying to herself.

You're stupid. Why do you care about him, anyway? Why do you care about any boy? You're a scientist. You're going to be a vet. Boys are a waste of time. You despise girls who are boy-crazy.

Despite her denials, she knew if he tried to kiss her, she'd let him. And she also knew she'd give anything in the world to go to the eighth-grade dance with him.

Adam Marino's office was totally different from what Kate would have imagined it to be. She'd envisioned plush leather chairs, highly polished dark woods, thick carpets. Instead, she discovered an airy suite with light oak, lots of green plants and brightly upholstered contemporary furniture.

Adam Marino himself, though, was exactly as she'd pictured him. Rising to greet her, his smile caused butterflies to erupt in her stomach. He was dressed impeccably in a charcoal-gray suit, pale blue shirt, gray-and-blue-striped silk tie. Although Kate didn't know much about the cost of men's clothing, even she could tell the suit alone had probably cost more than her entire monthly food budget.

His thick, dark hair was razor cut and, except for a recalcitrant lock that refused to stay put, looked model-perfect. And those eyes.

Kate swallowed. She'd been told about his gray eyes, how they looked like rain, how just one look caused even women who declared themselves immune to good-looking men to swoon. Telling herself to act her age, she accepted his handshake, giving him a firm one in return.

"How can I help you, Mrs. Bishop?" he asked after she was settled.

His admiring glance told Kate he approved of her carefully chosen outfit of her best black slacks, fitted white blouse, and just-purchased dark-red silk wool jacket. "I've just won the lottery," she said, although she could see this wasn't a surprise to him when he nodded. She went on to explain that she wanted, first of all, a new will. "After that, maybe you could advise me of other steps I might take that will safeguard my children."

"I'm flattered that you thought of me," he said, smiling again. "And I'll be happy to help you. But I'm not a financial expert."

"I know that. I have an appointment tomorrow to see Keith Ambrose of Ambrose & Associates in Austin. They come highly recommended."

"I've heard a number of good things about Ambrose & Associates."

His words were reassuring.

"I have a confession to make," he added. "When my secretary told me you'd called, I figured it was because of the lottery win, so I did some research this morning."

Kate smiled. People were right about Adam Marino. He wasn't just a pretty face.

"And in addition to a financial advisor, you're going to need a good accountant."

"But won't Ambrose & Associates have an accountant there?"

"I'm sure they do, but you'll be better off to have a three-pronged team that are not related: a top-notch attorney—" He grinned. "That's me. A top-notch financial advisor. And a top-notch accountant."

That made sense.

"And I'd make sure my team agreed before I did anything that had to do with spending a large chunk of money. Normal fees for services rendered are one thing. Investments, endowments, irrevocable trusts, family limited trusts, even gifts to friends and family— are quite another. From what I read, lots of lottery winners have ended up losing everything because of bad advice and too-quick decisions."

"I know," Kate said. "I've read the same things. I don't intend to be one of those people."

His expression turned thoughtful. "You seem sensible and grounded. Even so, you might want to consider talking to a counselor about all the changes in your life. Just the requests for money that'll probably come from people you care about are going to take an emotional toll, especially if you decide to turn them down."

Kate thought about Mel and the trip she'd suggested. She also thought about the cars she intended to buy and how she'd said she'd pay off Linda's charge cards and how she'd buy the building Linda was leasing. "That's probably a good idea. I-I've already made a number of promises to my family and my best friend."

"Do you regret them?"

Kate shook her head. "No, not really. But I can see how, under pressure, I might promise something I really *don't* want to do."

"Then I have another suggestion. From now on, when someone asks you for something that you find it hard to say 'no' to—especially if it's something you know you'll never want to do—just tell them all requests have to go through me."

Kate smiled. "Let you be the bad guy."

"Exactly."

"What if the person doing the requesting is one of my sisters or another family member I don't want to hurt or alienate?"

"Then it'll be even more important that you tell them I'm handling everything for you. If it'll make it easier for you, we can set some arbitrary amount—say any request that involves more than five thousand dollars has to go through me and your financial advisory team."

Thinking of all her millions, Kate said, "Five thousand isn't much."

"If you give away enough five-thousand-dollar gifts,

you'll be amazed at how fast the total adds up." His gaze was sympathetic. "But in the end, it is your money, and you don't have to ask anyone's permission to give it all away, if you're so inclined."

"I know."

"Just remember, anytime you're not sure what you want to do, just say you'll take it under advisement."

For the next half hour, they discussed the provisions she wanted in her will, and he suggested others that made sense, too. As she got ready to leave, she said, "I don't suppose you could recommend a good accountant?"

"I've worked with several I consider excellent. I'll have Theresa—my secretary—give you a list."

"Thank you." She stood after retrieving her purse from the floor where she'd set it earlier.

He stood, too, walking around his desk to escort her out. At the door he stopped before opening it, and their eyes met. Kate felt that flutter in her stomach again. He was way too good-looking and way too sexy. It was going to be hard to keep her thoughts on business when she was around him. And yet she was already looking forward to their working together. Thank God fantasies were harmless.

The silence stretched, becoming almost uncomfortable, yet Kate couldn't seem to move.

Then, shocking her, he said, "I never date clients."

Her heart knocked painfully. Had she been so transparent? Could he tell what she'd been thinking? She could feel her face flushing red.

"But I'm tempted to ignore my own rule," he added softly, his glance straying to her mouth.

For the life of her, Kate couldn't think of a thing to say. She felt like a teenager being noticed for the first time by the most popular boy in high school.

"Would you consider going out with me?" he added even more softly.

"I—" She wet her lips. And from somewhere came the perfect answer. "I'll have to take it under advisement."

As she drove home, she thought about how he'd laughed and said, "You learn fast." But he'd also squeezed her hand, adding, "If you decide your answer is yes, it'll definitely be worth breaking my rule."

"He didn't!"

"He did."

"Adam Marino wants to take you out? And you didn't say yes immediately?"

Kate laughed. "Linda, he's nine years younger than I am."

"So?"

"So what's the point?"

"What's the *point*? Are you *serious*? The best-looking and most eligible guy in town, a guy every woman who's ever set eyes on him would *kill* to spend time with, asks you to go out with him, and you don't see the *point*?"

Kate sighed. "I admit it's very tempting, but I'm not a masochist. I'm afraid of how he makes me feel, and I'm also a realist. Adam Marino would never pick someone like me for any kind of ongoing, serious relationship." She wanted to add that the insidious thought that her sudden wealth might have something to do with his interest in her had wormed its ugly way into her mind, but she hated to give voice to it, as if saying it out loud might prove it to be true. It was nicer to think that he really *was* attracted to her, even if she never took the relationship any further.

"Kate, you're crazy. Even if all you ever have with him is a few terrific dates and some no-strings, mind-blowing sex, what's the harm? You're single. You're over twenty-one. You're allowed to enjoy yourself."

"Who says sex with Adam Marino would be mind-blowing?"

Linda laughed. "God, all you have to do is look at him and you know it would be!"

"Sometimes gorgeous guys are selfish and think only of themselves," Kate countered.

"Who says?"

"*Cosmopolitan* magazine."

"You read that?"

"Not in front of the kids."

"I read it, too," Linda said sheepishly.

Kate hooted. "We're a pair, aren't we?"

"That's what happens when you're sex-starved."

"I'm not sex-starved." But the truth was, Kate did think about sex more and more often lately. It had been a long time, and she was a normal woman. Just the thought of sex with Adam Marino made her press her legs together.

"Then there's something wrong with you," Linda said.

"Well," Kate conceded, "I do think about it. But I'm not desperate."

"I'm about to the point where I'm thinking of buying a BOB."

"You wouldn't!" Kate could just imagine what the gossips would say if she bought a vibrator. She wasn't even sure where she'd *find* one in Cranbrook.

"Of course, I'd have to drive to Austin to get it," Linda said, chuckling, "or else I'd probably be run out of town. Not to mention how scandalized my mother would be!"

"Maybe your mother has a vibrator of her own."

At that, they burst out laughing again. Because the picture of nearly eighty-year-old Beverly Josephson—who was a pillar of the Cranbrook Community Church and the most straitlaced and puritanical person they knew, someone who even regarded *People* magazine as sinful—giving herself sexual pleasure, was hilarious.

"We shouldn't talk about your mom that way," Kate said when their laughter had subsided.

"Oh, I know, she's a good old egg. She's just so *rigid*."

"She can't help it."

"Quit being so damned nice, Kate. You don't have to be nice anymore. You're rich."

"Will you please be serious?"

"Okay, fine. Here's me, being serious. If you don't go out with Adam Marino and, in particular, if you don't have sex with him if he wants to, then you're either stupid or crazy."

Kate rolled her eyes, even though they were talking on the phone and Linda couldn't see her doing it.

"And stop rolling your eyes!" Linda said.

"You know me too well," Kate said dryly.

"No one has to know if you don't want them to," Linda went on, and this time she sounded very serious. "You can insist on going to a hotel in Austin where you'll be anonymous. Tell him as the mother of four impressionable children, you have to watch your reputation."

"Look, all of this is moot, anyway. Let's say I do go out with him. Maybe he'll be bored silly and not want to see me again."

"He'll want to see you again."

"I don't see how you can be so sure."

"Kate, quit putting yourself down. You're a very attractive, sexy woman. And you're smart and funny and interesting. Not to mention rich. He'll want to see you again."

Since Linda had brought up the subject of the money, Kate said, "Maybe it's the money that interests him and not me."

"Oh, c'mon, a woman can tell when a man is attracted to her. Anyway, he has money of his own. Gossip has it that old man Marino is worth a few million himself. And Adam's his golden-haired son."

"His hair is black."

"Figuratively speaking."

"You know, we could talk about this for hours and never get anywhere, but it'll have to be saved for another day because it's time for me to leave and pick up the girls."

"Okay. Are we still on for shopping Saturday?"

"That might have to wait till next week. I want to go look at cars on Saturday."

"Oh. Okay."

"One of those cars is going to be for you, but I won't make any decisions till you have a chance to look at it, too."

"You'd better not. It isn't every day I get a new car. Call me later, okay? I'll be home by ten."

Of everyone, Kate reflected as she drove to the girls' respective schools, Linda was the only person who still treated her the same way she'd always treated her. Yet Kate couldn't help but wonder how long that would last. Was it inevitable that their relationship would gradually change, too?

God, Kate hoped not. What would she do without Linda's sane outlook, her ability to laugh at herself and, better yet, make Kate laugh at *herself*, but most of all, her unwavering friendship and support?

CHAPTER 7

"Tessa, do you need a ride home tonight?"

The speaker was Frankie Amendola, a waiter at the Cranbrook Café where Tessa had worked for the past year.

"Thanks, Frankie, but Tom's picking me up."

"You sure? I mean, you could call him and tell him you've got a ride."

Stifling a sigh, she said, "He's probably already on his way." Tessa knew Frankie had a crush on her. It was obvious to anyone who saw the way he looked at her. Because she had a kind heart and hated hurting anyone's feelings, she always tried to let him down gently, but lately that had been getting more and more difficult to do.

The expectant light in Frankie's dark eyes dimmed. "Oh, okay." He seemed about to say something else, but, after hesitating a few moments, continued wiping down the tables and stacking the chairs in the corner in preparation for mopping the floor.

Ordinarily, Tessa would have helped him, even

though as hostess/cashier, it wasn't part of her job to clean up after they closed at night. Once she'd balanced out the register, tallied the credit card receipts and prepared the bank deposit, she was free to go. Tonight, though, she just wanted to get out of there. She was tired; it had been a long week.

She was also excited and anxious for tomorrow to come, because tomorrow her mom was taking her and Tom shopping for new cars. Tessa grinned. She'd never had a car of her own, let alone a new one. She knew her mom would probably want to buy them something sensible like a Toyota Corolla or a Honda Civic, but Tessa was thinking more in terms of a Jeep SUV or a sporty convertible. Wouldn't it be cool to drive a BMW or a Jag? Her friends would die of envy.

"You want to go see a late movie after work tomorrow night?

Tessa jumped. She hadn't heard Frankie's approach. "Um, I…I don't think I can." *Shoot. Why didn't I just say I already had plans?* "I, um, think my mom wants me to go to this thing with her." She almost moaned, hearing herself. She sounded so stupid. Any idiot would see through *that* flimsy excuse. What kind of *thing* started after ten? Especially one her *mother* would go to.

Damn. She avoided Frankie's eyes. Why did he have to look at her like a sad puppy and make her feel guilty even though she had no reason to feel guilty? After all, there was no law saying she had to go out with whomever asked her. And why wouldn't he take the hint? She'd refused him half a dozen times already.

Still not looking at him, she ducked down and re-trieved her purse from the shelf under the counter. When she stood up again, she heard a knock on the front window, and she saw Tom waving to her. "My brother's here," she said. "I've gotta go. See you tomorrow."

Frankie started to answer but Tessa didn't wait. She just waved and made her escape.

"Hey," Tom said. "You didn't have to hurry. I just wanted you to know I was here."

"I'm so glad. I couldn't wait to get out of there."

"Rough night?"

"No, not really. It's just Frankie again."

Tom made a face. "He still trying to get you to go out with him?"

Tessa nodded grimly. "He just won't take the hint."

"That's because he's in looooooove." He dragged out the word while making adoring cow eyes.

Tessa punched his arm. "Stop that!"

Tom laughed. "I'm sorry. Actually, I'm sorry for the poor guy. I know what it's like to be rejected, and believe me, it's not any fun."

"I've never encouraged him, Tom."

"I know that."

By now they'd reached Tom's beat-up old Subaru. He unlocked the passenger door and Tessa climbed in. She sighed in grateful relief to be off her feet. That was the hardest part of her job—standing for hours on end. Even though she wore the most comfortable shoes she owned, her feet still hurt at quitting time.

"Frankie's not so bad, you know," Tom said as he started the car.

"I know, but I'm just not *attracted* to him." In fact, the thought of Frankie touching her made her shudder.

"Look, I'm not criticizing you. Call it scientific curiosity or something, but what, exactly, is wrong with him?"

Tessa thought about the question. Frankie was actually fairly good-looking, and unlike a lot of the guys she knew, he was also ambitious. He attended Texas State University in San Marcos, cramming twelve class hours into three days a week while working most of the remaining four days. "There's really nothing wrong with him. I just…I don't feel that *spark*."

Tom braked for a red light and looked over at her.

"You understand, don't you?" she asked. "I mean, remember how you felt about Kelly Jeffers?"

"Oh, yeah, Kelly…"

Kelly had asked Tom to the senior prom and because he didn't have a girlfriend and Kelly was lively and pretty, he had said yes.

He'd admitted later that it had been a mistake to take her out. He'd known up front that he wasn't interested in her, but he'd figured what the heck—it was just a dance, she needed a date, he needed a date, they'd have a good time and that would be it.

It was soon clear Kelly didn't feel that way. She kept calling him and bumping into him "accidentally" at school. She had an "extra" ticket to a Black Eyed Peas concert—tickets that were almost impossible to get—and she invited him. It got harder and harder for Tom to avoid her, and finally he'd had to come out and tell her he wasn't interested in dating her. He'd been nice about it—Tom could hardly be any other way—but Kelly hadn't taken the rejection well.

She started spreading stories about him. She told people he'd expected sex after the prom and when she'd refused, he hadn't liked it. She said he was stalking her. Most of the people she told these lies to were people who knew Tom, and the majority of them didn't believe her. Still, the experience had left a bad taste in Tom's mouth and it had infuriated Tessa, because she'd always liked Kelly. Had, in fact, kind of pressed her case with Tom, saying he hadn't really given her a chance.

"You're right," Tom said now, patting her knee. "Maybe you need to come right out and tell him the truth, the way I did with her. Or," he added, giving her a sheepish look, "you could just take the easy way out and tell him you're already going out with someone."

"He'd know I was lying. He's heard me talking to Jenna." Jenna's dad owned the café, and she and Tessa had become good friends in the past year.

"Well, I guess you'll figure it out," Tom said.

"So how're things with Lucy?" Tessa asked after a few minutes. Lucy Robinson was Tom's girlfriend of the last few months.

"Okay."

Tessa frowned. "You don't sound too sure."

Tom shrugged and flipped his right turn signal on. "I don't know. She's...kind of intense."

Tessa couldn't read his expression in the dimness of the car. "What does that mean?"

He didn't answer for a few seconds. Then he blew out a breath. "I just think...hell, I don't know. She keeps hinting about getting married."

"Getting *married?* Geez, Tom. Have you given her any reason to think you might want to?"

"Not in *my* mind."

"I thought Lucy had three more years of school and that she really wanted to be a teacher."

"She does. But lately she's been talking about dropping out. And the other night she hinted about following me this fall when I go to flight school."

"Do you think the money has anything to do with this?"

Tom shook his head. "I could be wrong, but I don't think so." He gave an embarrassed laugh. "She's been like this for a while. Even before Mom won the lottery."

"Well, how do you feel? Would you want her to go with you?"

"Oh, hell," he muttered. "I don't know how I feel. I mean, I care about her, but I'm too young to get serious about anybody. The last thing I want to do is get married. And the truth is, when and if I get accepted into a flight school, I'd like to be free to concentrate on that and nothing else."

Tessa understood. She felt the same way. Right now, she had all she could do to handle her classes and prepare her required portfolio, drawings and application for RISD. They had to be submitted by mid-February for her to have a prayer of getting into the school for the fall semester. A romantic entanglement would only complicate her life.

Tom slowed as they approached their house. Tessa saw the light in their mother's bedroom go out and she smiled. Kate could never seem to go to sleep until all her kids were safe and accounted for. She'd kind of gotten over that where Tom and Tessa were concerned—after all, they were nineteen—but since she'd won the lottery she'd reverted back to being a mother hen and worrying about them constantly. Tessa guessed she understood. They'd certainly had their share of weird people hanging around and trying to squeeze money out of them.

Actually—and this disappointed Tessa—a couple of her friends had hinted that they could use a loan. Tessa had to laugh. A loan. As if they'd ever pay the money back if Tessa *were* to give them any. After the third one had said something to her, she'd finally had to tell them what her mother had said: that all requests for money had to go through her mom's lawyer. That had shut Tessa's so-called friends up pretty fast.

Tom pulled into the driveway and cut the engine. For a moment, neither of them moved, then they both opened their respective doors at the same time.

"I'm gonna make myself a peanut butter and jelly sandwich," Tom said once they'd entered the kitchen. "Want one?"

"Thanks, but I'm not hungry. I'm going to bed. We've got a big day tomorrow."

"Yeah. I've been looking at cars online, trying to make up my mind what I want." He took two slices of bread out of the loaf on the counter, then opened the cupboard and reached for the jar of peanut butter.

"You know Mom probably has ideas of her own about what she wants us to have."

Tom opened the utensil drawer and took out a knife. "Don't worry about that. I can handle Mom."

Tessa smiled. Although they'd seemingly dropped the subject of Lucy, she couldn't get Tom's dilemma out of her mind and knew she'd keep stewing over it until she told him what was on her mind. Hoping he wouldn't take it the wrong way, she said, "Tom, I know you didn't ask for my advice, but I'm going to give it anyway. I think you need to tell Lucy how you feel. It's not fair to keep seeing her if she's thinking marriage and you're thinking fun and sex for now, but that's it."

He unscrewed the lid on the jar of peanut butter and didn't answer.

Tessa cringed inwardly. She hated it when Tom got mad at her.

But then he surprised her by simply nodding. "You're right. I guess I've just been too chicken." His eyes finally met hers. "I didn't want to hurt her feelings. Or have to go through an ugly scene."

"Yeah, I know."

"I guess I'll tell her next week."

"Why wait? Aren't you seeing her this weekend?"

He made a face. "Yeah, we're going out Saturday night."

"Why not just tell her then?"

He sighed. "Saturday's her birthday. How can I tell her on her birthday?"

As Tessa headed for her room, she thought about how glad she was that she wasn't in Tom's shoes.

Kate was ready to scream. Never had she imagined that her sensible twins would give her so much grief over cars. Kate realized now that she'd probably been naive to imagine that Tom and Tessa would be happy to have a practical compact car with good gas mileage when they knew perfectly well that she could afford to buy them the sporty SUVs and convertibles they wanted.

After half a day of stalemate, she finally gave in and allowed Tessa to choose a dark-blue BMW convertible and Tom to take possession of a silver Toyota 4Runner SUV. In the same spirit of "why not?", she bought herself a gorgeous champagne Lexus.

But that experience told her she had no desire to go shopping for anyone else. Instead, she would tell each person in her family, as well as Linda and Mark, that they could choose a vehicle that cost $35,000 or less and she would pay for it. Anything that cost more than that, the recipient would have to pay the difference.

"Period. End of discussion," she said to Melissa, who actually tried to argue with her. Apparently the model Mel had picked out was considerably more expensive than the allotment from Kate.

"It's not like you can't afford it," Mel said peevishly.

"That's not the point. I have to draw the line somewhere."

Later, talking to Linda—who was the only one who *hadn't* complained, Kate said, "You'd think they'd all be thrilled to have *any* new car, wouldn't you? I just can't believe how *greedy* they're all acting."

Linda gave her a cynical smile. "Can't you?"

Kate frowned. "What do you mean?"

"I mean, it's human nature to want more. We're never satisfied. Look at the stock market debacle in 2000. Up to that point, everyone was making tons of money. People who'd never been in the market were suddenly players. Shoot, I jumped in myself. I actually borrowed money against my house and bought tech stocks, because I wanted to make a killing the way some of my friends were. Then, even after I'd made a nice profit, I didn't sell. Why? Because I wanted more. And you know what eventually happened…."

Kate nodded grimly. "Yeah, everyone lost their shirts." Then she sighed. "I just hope this isn't going to keep up. You know, I really thought my family would be *grateful* when I said I was buying everyone a new car. Instead, they just seem to expect this as their due."

"Try to put yourself in their place," Linda said. "What if, say, Joanna had won instead of you? Wouldn't you expect her to share with you?"

Kate thought about that for a while, finally saying, "Yes, I guess you're right."

"Your mom was happy with your choice of car for her, though, wasn't she?"

Kate smiled. Harriet had surprised her again. "Yes, she was thrilled, actually."

"I'm thrilled, too," Linda said.

"I know you are."

"I'll never be able to thank you enough for what you've done for me."

"I don't need thanks. You'd have done the same for me, and I know it." Kate hesitated. "Um, there's only one thing."

Linda raised her eyebrows. "You want my firstborn."

Kate laughed. "No, but I do have a favor to ask of you."

"Anything."

"Um, don't say anything about me buying that building for you, okay? Or anything about the credit cards."

Linda nodded thoughtfully.

Kate knew Linda understood why the request had been made. Kate didn't need to explain that Joanna, in particular, would be upset to know what Kate had done for Linda. It was sad that Joanna was so jealous of their relationship, but some things never changed. It also wouldn't matter that Kate intended to do a lot more for Joanna and her family. Her sister would always be envious of Kate's relationship with Linda.

"Would you ladies like to see the dessert menu?"

Kate and Linda looked up. They had just finished dinner at a popular Italian restaurant on the outskirts of San Marcos.

Linda looked at Kate.

"Better not," Kate said.

"Just bring us the bill," Linda said.

Later, after settling the bill, which Kate insisted upon paying, the two friends were oddly silent on the way home. Finally Linda said, "I don't know what I'd do without you, Kate."

Kate cast her a sidelong glance. "I feel the same way."

"I just don't want—" She stopped.

Kate frowned. "What?"

"I don't want things to change between us."

Kate turned onto Linda's street. "Why should they change?"

Linda shrugged. "Your life is already changing."

Kate sighed. "I know. But the changes won't affect *us*, will they?"

"I hope not," Linda answered softly.

"But why would they? Unless...does it *bother* you that I have all this money now?"

Linda hesitated. "I know it shouldn't, but it's beginning to."

"Linda!"

"I know, I know. I shouldn't let it make a difference, but I can see that your life is going to go in a different direction than mine, and I'm just afraid we'll grow apart."

By now Kate had reached Linda's house and pulled into the drive. "We won't grow apart if we don't want to."

"We may not be able to prevent it."

"I don't know why you say that."

"I can't help it. I can already see that you'll probably move away from Cranbrook."

"I have no intention of moving away. Everyone I love is here."

"I know you feel that way now, but after a few months of being constantly hassled about the money, you may decide you need distance from your family."

Kate wanted to dispute this, but Linda had a valid point. Kate had *already* gotten tired of the way her sisters were acting. The way *everyone* was acting. Except for Linda, she amended. "Even if I did decide to move somewhere else, you will always be my best friend."

Linda nodded, but she didn't seem convinced.

"You *will* be. Nothing can *ever* change that."

"It won't be the same if you're not here, though."

Kate sighed. "Look, this is all just speculation, anyway. Like I said, I have no intention of leaving Cranbrook. If that changes, we'll deal with it then. Okay?" When Linda didn't immediately answer, Kate said more insistently, *"Okay?"*

Linda finally turned and met Kate's eyes. "Okay."

But as Kate drove home and replayed the conversation in her mind, she knew Linda still wasn't convinced. And the truth was, Kate wasn't convinced, either. Because Linda was right. If Kate ended up having to leave Cranbrook, everything *would* change.

Whether Kate wanted it to or not.

CHAPTER 8

Kate liked Keith Ambrose immediately. With his thick brown hair, hazel eyes and nice, solid build, he gave off an aura of dependability. He looked to be about fifty—later she would find out he was actually forty-nine. She'd expected to be intimidated because she knew he was extremely successful, but strangely, she felt entirely comfortable with him from the moment she was shown into his Austin office.

"It's a great pleasure to meet you," he said, rising as she entered. He walked around his desk and shook her hand. "You're the first lottery winner I've ever worked with."

"That makes us even," Kate said with a smile, "because you're the first financial advisor I've ever worked with."

He invited her to have a seat in one of the comfortable-looking leather chairs in front of his desk, offered her something to drink—which she declined—then sat down at his desk and reached for a thick folder.

For the next hour, he talked to her about possible investment options, showing her various charts and analyses. Then he made his recommendations.

Kate's head was spinning by the time he'd finished.

Seeing the expression on her face, he chuckled. "Don't worry. I've got copies of everything we've talked about today. You can take them home, study them, and think about what I've said. I don't expect you to remember all this, and I don't expect you to make snap decisions. In fact, I strongly advise against that."

Kate nodded.

"But I wouldn't wait too long before deciding how you want to invest. The money isn't working for you just sitting in your bank."

"I know."

"Plus, it's too easy to spend it right now." He smiled. "Best to get it tied up so you won't be tempted to make impulse buys."

Kate thought about what she'd already spent and/or promised to spend, which was quickly adding up. "That sounds like good advice."

"I'm also including a copy of our fee structure here, so you'll know up front how much you're going to be paying for our services."

Kate took the file he'd put together for her and stood. "Thank you so much. I'll give you a call after I've had a chance to look everything over."

"Good. But don't rush off. I'd like to take you to lunch."

"Thank you, but I can't. I have another appointment in less than an hour." Kate was meeting with one of the accountants recommended by Adam Marino.

"That's too bad. I was looking forward to getting to know you better."

The warmth of his expression made Kate feel uncomfortable. Did he ask *all* his clients to lunch? Or was he flirting with her?

"Since you can't go today, I hope you'll allow me to buy you lunch the next time we meet."

"I'd enjoy that," Kate said. She wondered what was wrong with her. Why had she thought he was flirting with her? He was just being nice.

You thought so because you wanted to think so. The truth is, you're attracted to him, aren't you?

Even the thought made her face feel warmer. Maybe Linda had been right. Maybe she *was* sex-starved. She couldn't imagine any other reason for her to suddenly start seeing every man she met as desirable.

First Adam Marino.

And now Keith Ambrose.

But if she was going to be interested in someone, at least Keith Ambrose was a more sensible choice than Adam Marino.

Wasn't he?

"Hey, Nic, wait up!"

Nicole, who was on her way to study hall, turned at the sound of her best friend, Tracy's, voice. As usual, Tracy's red hair looked wild, as if she hadn't combed it in a week.

"Where you going?" Tracy said, breathing fast. She carried fifteen extra pounds, which she was always trying to diet off.

"Study hall," Nicole said. She flipped her own dark, straight hair back. "Don't you have Spanish?"

"I'm cutting."

"You're *cutting?* Where are you going?"

Tracy lowered her voice, although there was so much noise in the hall, no one could have heard her, anyway. "I'm meeting Aaron behind the bleachers."

"Trace, you're gonna get in trouble."

Tracy shrugged. "I don't care." Her eyes, brown flecked with gold, met Nicole's. "I love him, Nic."

Nicole refrained from rolling her eyes. She couldn't understand how Tracy—an honor student bound for UT when she graduated—could have become so stupid over a boy, especially one like Aaron Fielding, who Nicole considered a conceited jerk who never thought about anyone but himself. He probably wanted Tracy to meet him out there to suck him off, and she'd do it, too. She'd already admitted to Nicole that she'd done it to him in the backseat of his brother's car. That had made Nicole sick, because she could just see Aaron Fielding watching them in the rearview mirror. And then telling all his friends.

"I'm sure he's going to ask me to the spring dance," Tracy said now, eyes shining.

Nicole nodded, but she wasn't as sure as Tracy seemed to be. Nicole had seen Aaron walking with his arm around Lisa Blake earlier today, and last week she'd seen him push Candice Short up against her locker, then stand so close to her they were touching. She wondered if she should tell Tracy, but something held her back. Tracy wouldn't believe her. She'd just think Nicole was jealous because she didn't have a boyfriend of her own. *Was* she jealous? It was true Nic wanted a boyfriend, but not someone like Aaron. She wanted someone nice. Someone smart. Someone who could talk to her and someone *she* could talk to. She sure didn't want someone who only wanted her for one thing.

Nicole was still a virgin. She'd never even had oral sex, which a lot of the kids seemed to think wasn't really having sex at all.

"I saw this *gorgeous* dress in the window of Lana's Shop," Tracy was now saying. "Have you seen it? It's black and has sequins around the top, the waist and the hem."

Nicole *had* seen it, and it *was* gorgeous. She'd even thought it was just the kind of dress she'd wear to the spring dance if, by some miracle, someone asked her.

"So I was wondering…can you lend me the money to buy it?"

"Huh?" Nicole said, blinking. The question had thrown her.

"It's only two hundred dollars."

"Where would *I* get two hundred dollars?"

Tracy looked at her as if she had two heads. "Well, duh. From your mother. Where else?"

"Trace, I can't ask my mother for two hundred dollars. She'd want to know why I needed it. What would I *say*?"

"Oh, c'mon. Your mother has *millions*. Why would she care?"

"Well, she *would* care. Anyway, just because she won that money doesn't mean I have any of it. Besides, where would you get the money to pay me back?"

Tracy just looked at her.

It took a few moments for Nicole to realize Tracy hadn't really meant *lend* me the money. She'd meant *give* me the money. Nicole shrugged. "I'm sorry, Tracy. But my mom wouldn't give me the money even if I *did* ask."

Tracy didn't immediately answer. When she did, her voice was hard. "You're jealous of me and Aaron, aren't you?"

The unfairness of the accusation stung Nicole. "That's not a very nice thing to say. Besides, I'm not the least bit jealous."

Tracy's expression was disdainful. "Yes, you are. You're green because *you* don't have a boyfriend. I thought you were my friend. My *best* friend."

Just then, the warning bell rang, which meant they had exactly sixty seconds to get out of the hall and into whatever classroom they were headed for.

Nicole swallowed. "I have to go. I'll talk to you later." Her eyes had filled with tears, and she angrily brushed them away as she hurried off. She couldn't believe Tracy was acting like this. A couple other of

Nicole's friends had hinted about money in the past week, but no one had come right out and asked her for any. And to think Tracy had. Tracy. Her best friend.

My former best friend.

For the rest of the day Nicole thought about Tracy and the way she had acted. She wished it didn't hurt so much, but it did. *Mom's right. I've got to toughen up.* Her mother was always telling her that, saying Nicole was too sensitive.

"Honey," she'd said only the other day, "if you're serious about a career in music, you're going to have to develop a thicker skin. It's a really tough business and there's lots of rejection."

Thinking about Juilliard and all the opportunities she would have that most of the kids she knew could only dream about, Nicole decided she wasn't going to let Tracy get to her. Tracy could say whatever she wanted and she could do whatever she wanted. From now on, Nicole couldn't care less.

In fact, she would find herself a new best friend.

Melissa was shocked by how much money the Slaters wanted for the restaurant. Sure, she'd known the property on the lake was valuable and that the restaurant had a good clientele, but two million?

"You seem surprised," Bucky Spencer said.

"Well, it's not like Slater's is located in *Austin*," Mel said. "I mean, it's kind of in the boonies."

"What you call the boonies is quickly becoming the most desirable property in the county. The lakefront lot alone is worth nearly a million," Bucky said. "Then there's the building and all the equipment, not to mention the goodwill. Believe me, this is a very fair asking price. Personally, if Slater's belonged to me, I'd ask even more."

"If it's worth so much, why don't Connie and Whit *ask* more?"

"If you're serious about buying the place, you ought to be glad they aren't," Bucky said. He leaned back in his chair and stuck his thumbs behind his suspenders, pushing them out. He always wore suspenders, usually red ones.

The affectation amused Mel, who figured he probably thought the suspenders made him look like Atticus Finch or something. He regarded her thoughtfully. "*Are* you serious?"

"Yeah, but—" Mel took a deep breath. "I'm not sure I can raise that much money."

Bucky smiled knowingly. "Hell, Mel, we all know about Kate's winnings. Sure you can."

Some sense of self-preservation made Mel say, "I haven't decided if I'm going to ask her or not. I want to go over everything first."

"Don't take too long," Bucky warned. "There are other buyers interested."

Mel studied him for a long moment, trying to decide if he was giving her a line of bull or if there really *were* other potential buyers. But his expression gave away nothing. Affectations aside, Bucky really was a good lawyer as well as a good poker player. And today he wore his poker face.

"Can I have copies of those?" she finally said, gesturing to the file containing the restaurant's financial records, a list of its inventory and the Slaters' existing contracts with vendors.

"Certainly." Bucky pressed a buzzer and when his secretary answered, said, "Darlene, could you come in here, please?"

Thirty minutes later, armed with all the information she'd requested, Mel left Bucky's office and headed home. She wished she had a handle on how Kate would react when she told her about the restaurant and what she wanted to do. In the end, though, there was probably only one way to find out, and that was to take the plunge and ask.

Surely she won't refuse. Not with all that money. In fact, she's probably planning to give each of us a couple of million dollars, maybe even three million apiece. Buying the restaurant for me will actually be cheaper for her! That's it. That'll be my strategy. I'll tell her if she buys Slater's for me, she won't have to give me anything else. Well, except for my car, but she's already doing that.

By the time she reached her apartment, Mel felt a lot better. Kate wouldn't say no.

Mel would ask her tomorrow.

* * *

Tom was disgusted with himself.

He'd had the perfect opportunity to break it off with Lucy tonight, and at the last minute, he'd chickened out. Again.

What was wrong with him that he couldn't just *tell* her?

He'd always had this problem. He didn't like confrontation of any kind. It was probably a good thing he'd hadn't gotten into the Air Force Academy because down deep he knew he wasn't suited to the military. He'd let his fascination with flying cloud his judgment.

Sometimes now he wasn't even sure he wanted to go to flight school. Thing is, he'd still like to take flying lessons, but lately what he'd *really* been thinking he'd like to do was go to college and get a degree in landscaping design. He'd never have believed what he'd considered a means-to-an-end job this past year would turn out to be something that satisfied a part of him he hadn't even known was there. He'd done some research lately and knew he could get this course of study at several different Texas schools, but where he'd *really* like to go was Columbia University in New York.

And this summer, he'd like to backpack through Europe. See all the great gardens and parks in Italy and France and England. And drink beer in Germany, too, of course.

He grinned. He wondered if he could get his mom to go along with that plan. She'd be thrilled about school and landscape design, of course, but he wasn't sure about Columbia University or the European trip. Well, he could work on her. He had a while.

But first, he *had* to break things off with Lucy.

CHAPTER 9

Several days after Kate's meeting with Keith Ambrose, she got a call from Adam Marino's secretary saying her new will was ready to be signed.

Once again, Kate dressed carefully for her appointment the following day, this time wearing a new russet cashmere skirt and matching sweater paired with soft leather boots and an ecru crocheted shawl. Earlier, she'd had her hair cut in a shorter, more youthful style, and she'd even splurged on having it highlighted.

She'd also had a facial—her first ever—and spent more than an hour at the MAC counter at Nordstrom in Austin learning how to apply makeup so that it didn't look as if she was wearing any.

She knew she looked good, and because she knew it, she carried herself with more confidence, which made her look even better. It was amazing what new, expensive clothes, and new, expensive makeup and a new, expensive hairstyle could do for a woman.

And it all paid off.

Adam Marino was frankly admiring as he ushered

her into his office. She tried to hide her own admiration as she studied him surreptitiously. Today he wore a beautifully cut dark-navy suit paired with a snowy shirt and yellow tie. There really was something about a man in a suit...

And those eyes. Kate had found herself dreaming about those eyes several times since she'd last been here. He was entirely too attractive. As he rifled through the papers on his desk, she noticed how long and elegant his fingers were. A musician's fingers, she thought, wondering if he played an instrument. Idly, she imagined what those fingers would feel like on her body, then, appalled and afraid she was blushing, forced the thought away. Good grief! What was *wrong* with her?

Thankfully, just then he located the will he'd prepared for her signature and handed it to her, which helped her regain her composure.

"Look that over and make sure everything's okay before you sign it," he said. "When you're ready, I'll call my secretary and paralegal in to be witnesses."

Kate made herself read the will carefully. Once she was certain everything was the way she wanted it, she looked up. "It looks great."

Five minutes later, with Theresa, his secretary, and Darryl, his paralegal, watching, Kate signed the will.

After that, she only had to sign the power of attorney, giving Adam—with prior approval from both her financial advisor and her accountant—jurisdiction over her affairs should she become incapacitated, and she was finished.

"I'll walk you out," Adam said as she prepared to leave.

"Oh, that's not necess—"

"I want to," he said, cutting off her protest.

Kate's traitorous heart sped up at the warm look in his eyes.

"Back in a couple of minutes," he said to Theresa as they passed her desk.

Kate wondered what the secretary was thinking. Did Adam walk every client out when they left his office? Or was she getting special treatment?

When they reached the elevator, they were the only two there and, after pressing the Down button, Adam turned to her. "I'd still like to take you out sometime, Kate. Have you given it any more thought?"

Kate was proud of her even reply, which didn't betray the way her heart was skittering. "As a matter of fact, I have."

"And?"

"And I'd like that, too."

Just then the elevator dinged and the doors slid open. An older gentleman with a cane walked slowly off. Once he'd cleared the doors, Adam followed Kate on. He waited until the doors had closed before saying, "How about Friday night?"

Kate was finding it heard to breathe. "Friday's perfect."

He smiled. "Good. I thought I'd take you to the club for dinner."

The only times Kate had been to the Cranbrook Country Club were for weddings and once for an anniversary dinner. Immediately she began worrying about what she should wear.

When the elevator stopped at the lobby, Adam walked out with her. After telling her he'd pick her up at seven on Friday, they said goodbye.

Kate walked away self-consciously. She wanted, more than anything, to turn around and see if he was watching her, but she didn't want to give him the satisfaction of knowing she cared.

As she pushed the outside door open, she got her answer, for she could see Adam's reflection in the glass, and he *was* watching her.

Kate smiled all the way home.

Melissa hated that she was so nervous. *It's only Kate*, she kept telling herself. *What's the worst that can happen? She'll say no*.

But she wouldn't say no. Melissa would do such a great job of presenting her case, Kate couldn't possibly say no.

Kate was coming to Slater's for dinner tonight. Melissa had invited her, saying she wanted to talk to her about something really important, and she didn't want to do it at home.

"Wouldn't you rather go somewhere else on your day off?" Kate had asked.

"Slater's has the best food around," Mel had answered.

"You're right, of course. Do you want me to pick you up?"

Mel really wanted to drive herself. Even though she hadn't been able to persuade Kate to buy her a Corvette or something equally expensive, she was still getting a kick out driving a new car, even if it was just a Miata convertible.

A cute, red Miata convertible.

Mel smiled. Okay, so she hadn't gotten exactly what she wanted, but the Miata *was* adorable, low slung and sexy-looking. Actually, she couldn't wait for the weather to warm up so she could drive around with the top down. Make all the other women in town jealous.

But even though she wanted to drive to the restaurant, she decided maybe it would give her an advantage to allow Kate to drive tonight, so when Kate asked, Mel said, "Sure. How's six-fifteen? I'll make us a reservation for seven."

It was almost six-fifteen now.

Mel chewed on her lower lip and tried to decide whether to broach the subject of buying Slater's on the way there, at dinner or on the way home.

She quickly dismissed doing it on the way there. Best to reinforce how wonderful Slater's was by refreshing Kate's memory at dinner, *then* hitting her with the proposal. Mel had already alerted Janine, who was serving as the hostess in Connie's absence, to sit them in Evan's section. Evan was their best waiter, and Mel wanted everything to be perfect tonight.

"This is so nice," Kate said as they drank a pre-dinner glass of pinot noir. "Thank you for suggesting it."

"It's little enough to do as a thank-you," Mel said.

Kate smiled.

She looked really happy tonight, Mel thought. Way more relaxed than she'd been in a long time. Of course, having plenty of money would relax *anyone*. Nice not to have to worry about how you were going to pay the bills. And *really* nice to know no matter what you wanted you could have it. Mel tried not to feel envious, but it was hard. It would be so much nicer if *she* had won the money.

Kate ordered one of the specials—flounder stuffed with baby shrimp and crab meat—and Mel ordered one of Slater's famed New York strip steaks. She even decided the hell with her perpetual diet and told Evan she wanted French fries to go along with it. "And I want ranch dressing on my salad, and lots of it," she added.

Evan raised his eyebrows.

"My diet's taking a night off," Mel said.

Kate laughed. "Mine, too."

"Personally, I think both of you look great," Evan said.

Mel rolled her eyes. "Don't pay any attention to him. He tells that to all the women. Thinks we'll give him a bigger tip."

Evan grinned. "It works, too." Then he sobered. "I'll be back with your salads right away."

The sisters talked about their kids while they waited for their food. Kate admitted she was a bit worried about both Erin and Nicole.

This was news to Mel. Kate's girls never gave her fits the way Leeann did Mel. In fact, it was sometimes nauseating how perfect they were. "Why?" she asked.

Kate shrugged. "I don't know why. It's just that neither one seems herself. But when I've tried to talk to them about it, they both say nothing's wrong." She grimaced. "Nicole's favorite expression seems to be *don't worry about it.*"

Mel nodded sympathetically. "Leeann isn't even *that* nice," she admitted. "She just acts disgusted, as if I'm stupid or something."

Kate sighed. "Isn't it a good thing we don't know how hard it's going to be to raise them before we have them?"

"You can say that again. There'd be a lot fewer babies born, I can tell you that."

The discussion continued through the salad course, but when their entrées arrived, they gave their full attention to the food. Both entrées were wonderful. Kate raved about hers, even though she couldn't eat it all, and Mel relished every bite of hers.

Over coffee and a shared piece of caramel cheesecake, Mel decided the perfect time had arrived.

"Connie and Whit have put Slater's up for sale," she said.

Kate's mouth dropped open. *"Why?"*

So Mel explained about Whit's cancer.

"Oh, I'm so sorry," Kate said. "But why sell the restaurant?" She looked around. Although it was a weeknight, the restaurant was crowded. "It's so successful."

"I think they're tired. Even if Whit *wasn't* sick, they might have decided to sell."

"It might be harder than they imagine to give this up," she said thoughtfully. "I hope they're not sorry."

Mel waited a few moments, then said softly, "I want to buy the restaurant."

Kate blinked. A few seconds passed before light dawned in her eyes. "You mean you want *me* to buy it for you."

Mel couldn't see any point in hedging. "Well, yes, but—"

"Mel, you don't know anything about running a business. And from what I've heard, the restaurant business is probably one of the most risky to undertake."

"That's true for a new place, but Slater's is an *established* restaurant. It has a wonderful reputation and is extremely successful. The goodwill alone is priceless."

Kate stared at her, and Mel forced herself not to look away. "How much do they want?" she finally asked.

Mel wet her lips. "Two million."

"Two *million!*"

The people sitting nearest to them looked over at Kate's exclamation.

"Good heavens, Mel," Kate said in a lower voice. "Are you serious?"

"Of course I'm serious. This is the opportunity of a lifetime, Kate. A place like Slater's doesn't come on the market very often. Whoever buys it is buying a gold mine."

"You say that like it's just going to magically make money. Keeping a place like Slater's going takes extremely hard work, not to mention business savvy and tons of experience, none of which you have."

"I've worked in the restaurant business for years!"

"As a waitress."

"So? I know the business from the ground up."

"All you know about is waiting tables."

"I can learn the rest."

"Mel, listen to yourself. You're not making sense. Slater's needs someone who can jump in with both feet. Someone who knows the business inside and out." Her voice softened. "I'm sorry. But there's no way I can give you two million dollars."

"You mean you won't." Mel couldn't believe Kate was saying no.

"I'm sorry," Kate said again.

"This isn't some pie-in-the-sky thing I just thought of, Kate." Mel tried to keep the bitterness out of her voice. She knew if she attacked Kate, she'd completely ruin her chances. "I spent hours with Bucky Spencer. We went over all the books. All the financial statements. I have a formal proposal prepared. At least *read* it before you say no."

Kate sighed. "I'll tell you what, Mel. I've promised Adam Marino that any request that's over five thousand dollars is to be vetted through him, my financial advisor and my accountant. I'll give your proposal to them. If they think Slater's is a good investment, then I'll consider it."

"You're going to make me go through your *attorney?* I'm your *sister,* for crying out loud." Although Mel knew she'd probably be sorry, she couldn't seem to keep from saying, "I just can't believe how selfish you're being. Good grief, Kate, two million dollars is a drop in the bucket to you. Yet you're acting like I'm asking you to give me your last cent!"

The drive home was fraught with tension.

Neither sister spoke, and when Kate pulled up in front of Mel's apartment, Mel climbed out without a word.

As she walked inside, she didn't know if Kate was still there or if she'd already pulled away from the curb, and she didn't care.

From the moment she opened the door to Adam on Friday night, Kate had known the evening was going to be one to remember.

She had bought a new dress—short, red and sexy.

With it she wore a long rope of pearls and high black heels with pointy toes. Normally she avoided pointy toes because they weren't comfortable, but as Joanna had said more than once, a woman had to suffer to be beautiful.

And tonight Kate wanted to be beautiful.

"Wow," Adam said when he saw her. "Don't you look nice."

"You don't look so bad yourself." That was an understatement. He looked gorgeous. He could be a model for a GQ ad with his gray slacks, black sport coat and black silk shirt. In fact, Kate thought in flustered amusement, he should have a warning sign on his forehead: Danger Ahead.

If only he wasn't so much younger than her. Then again, it wasn't as if they were going to be married. This was just a date.

They didn't talk much on the drive to the country club. Adam had put a Sheryl Crow CD in the player, and they listened to the music with only an occasional comment on a song. Twenty minutes later, he pulled into the front turnaround and the attendant on duty opened the passenger door and helped Kate out. A moment later, hand tucked into Adam's arm, they climbed the steps to the entrance.

During dinner, a lot of people—a good many of them attractive women—came up to their table to speak to Adam. Although he was friendly, even charming, he never made Kate feel left out.

NO POSTAGE
NECESSARY
IF MAILED
IN THE
UNITED STATES

BUSINESS REPLY MAIL
FIRST-CLASS MAIL   PERMIT NO. 717-003   BUFFALO, NY

POSTAGE WILL BE PAID BY ADDRESSEE

HARLEQUIN READER SERVICE
3010 WALDEN AVE
PO BOX 1867
BUFFALO NY 14240-9952

Get FREE BOOKS and
FREE GIFTS when you play the...

LAS VEGAS
GAME

*Just scratch off
the gold box with a coin.
Then check below to see
the gifts you get!*

YES! I have scratched off the gold box. Please send me my **2 FREE BOOKS** and **2 FREE GIFTS** for which I qualify. I understand that I am under no obligation to purchase any books as explained on the back of this card.

355 HDL ELRQ   155 HDL ELV3

FIRST NAME

LAST NAME

ADDRESS

APT.#   CITY

STATE/PROV.   ZIP/POSTAL CODE

(H-N-03/07)

7	7	7
🍒	🍒	🍒
🔔	🔔	♣

Worth TWO FREE BOOKS plus
TWO BONUS Mystery Gifts!

Worth TWO FREE BOOKS!

TRY AGAIN!

www.eHarlequin.com

Offer limited to one per household and not
valid to current Harlequin® Next™
subscribers. All orders subject to approval.

"You seem to know everyone," Kate commented.

Adam shrugged. "I'm the mayor's son and I'm a lawyer."

You're also the most eligible bachelor around....

Thankfully, by the time their dessert arrived, they finally had a lull.

"So tell me about yourself," he said after their waiter had filled their coffee cups. "I know you have four children. How old are they?"

"Tessa and Tom—they're twins—are nineteen. Nicole is fifteen. And Erin is thirteen."

His smile seemed wistful. "It's funny. I thought by now I'd have a couple of kids of my own, but things didn't work out that way."

"You're still awfully young."

He gave her an odd look. "Not *that* young."

"You're nine years younger than I am." Might as well get it out in the open.

For a moment he didn't say anything. "Does that bother you, Kate?"

She took a sip of her coffee before answering. She wanted to be honest; on the other hand, she didn't want him to think she was assuming their relationship was more than it was. She decided to try for a light tone. "In a way."

"Don't let it. Nine years is nothing. Especially—" here he smiled "—when the woman in question is as attractive and desirable as you are."

Again, Kate wondered if it was *her* he found desirable or her money. And yet, if it was just her money that interested him, he was a darned good actor. "You'll make me blush."

He chuckled. "What's wrong? Can't take a compliment?"

"I'm not used to compliments."

"I find that hard to believe."

"It's true."

"The men in your life must be blind, then."

Kate smiled ruefully. "Maybe that's the problem. There haven't *been* any men in my life for a long time now."

"How long have you been divorced?"

"Almost seven years."

"Surely you're not saying you haven't dated in seven years."

"That's pretty much what I'm saying."

"But why not?"

"Truth? When you've got four kids and a full-time job, it leaves very little time or energy for dating."

He nodded thoughtfully. "I really admire women like you. I'm not sure I could have handled all that."

"You'd be surprised what you're capable of. When put to the test, most of us do what we have to do."

He considered her answer for a moment before speaking. Then, thoughtfully, he said, "I think women are a lot stronger and more resilient than men."

Kate thought so, too.

"Take my sister," he said. "Cathy's been battling lupus for the past two years—undergoing all kinds of painful treatments—yet you'd never know it to meet her. She's still working, and although she's slowed down, she's still caring for her family the way she always has."

"How old is she?"

"Forty."

"Do you have just the one sister?" Kate remembered hearing that there were several children in the Marino family.

"No, I have another, younger, sister, and an older brother. They don't live in Cranbrook, though. Jeff's in Dallas and Beth's in Atlanta." He smiled. "They're all married except me. And each has a pair of kids."

After that, the talk turned to more casual things, and before Kate knew it, the evening was over.

As they drove home, she began to worry about what would happen when they got to the house. Would he try to kiss her? Should she let him?

She needn't have worried. It wasn't awkward. He pulled into her driveway and cut the ignition, then got out and walked around to her side of the car. He took her hand and helped her out of the car, then walked her to the door.

"I had a wonderful time tonight," he said.

"I did, too. Thank you."

"I'd like us to do it again."

"I'd like that, too."

"Good." He smiled. "I'll call you." Then, before she could react, he pulled her close and kissed her.

Kate's head was spinning when he released her. Suddenly she wished she didn't have four children asleep inside. She knew she would have gone to bed with him if he'd asked, even though she still couldn't keep from wondering if he would have looked at her twice if not for the money.

When Kate got home from church on Sunday, there was a message waiting for her on her voice mail from her pastor.

"Kate, would you give me a call?" he said. "There's something I'd like to discuss with you."

Kate sighed. If Reverend Francis was like everyone else, the topic probably had something to do with her lottery winnings.

She put off calling him until two o'clock, figuring she could always say she'd gone out to lunch or something.

"Thank you for calling me so promptly," he said when he answered. "I'd hoped to catch you before you left the service today, but you were gone by the time I came outside."

"Yes, I had a brunch date," Kate fibbed smoothly.

"I was afraid maybe you'd be moving away and not coming to our church anymore," he said.

"I don't have any plans to do that."

"Wonderful." He paused for a moment. "You know we're going to be building a new church?"

"I'd heard that."

"We finalized the plans at our last meeting of the administrative council."

Here it comes. He definitely wants money.

"Anyway, Kate, that's where you come in. We talked about you at the meeting and everyone agrees how lucky we are that one of our very own is in such a good position to help us with a sizable donation."

Kate smiled. "Of course I'll help. I'll be happy to." She guessed neither Adam nor Keith would object to her donating, say, ten thousand dollars to the church building fund.

"I knew that's what you'd say, my dear. And God will surely bless you for it. The sum we had in mind is three million dollars."

Kate nearly dropped the phone. Three million dollars! Was he *serious?* When she finally found her voice, she said, "Although I'm happy to be one of the contributors, before I can pledge anything concrete, I would want to see the blueprints, estimates and any contracts that have been awarded. Once my attorney, financial advisor and accountant have looked everything over, we'll make a decision."

The pastor sputtered a bit, then reluctantly agreed to provide Kate with the documents she'd asked for.

It wasn't an hour later that her mother phoned. She was livid. "I can't believe you questioned Reverend Francis like that! Why, you could afford to pay the entire cost of building a new church."

"If I did everything everyone wants me to do, all twenty-eight million will be gone in a year," Kate said wearily.

"But this is the *church*."

"I know it's the church, Mother. But three million *dollars*? Don't you think that's excessive?"

"As Reverend Francis pointed out to me, it's no more than a tithe would be. Surely you are planning to give a sizable portion of your winnings to the church, anyway. Aren't you?"

"I don't know if I am or not. Look, I told Reverend Francis I'll be happy to contribute to the building fund. I just think what he's asking for is unreasonable."

"And you don't care that you're embarrassing me."

Kate closed her eyes. "There's no reason for you to be embarrassed. I'm only behaving like any sensible business person would behave. And if Reverend Francis objects, well then maybe the plans and estimates for the new church *need* review."

"The truth is," her mother said furiously, "you don't want to part with *any* of that money."

"Mom…"

"I know you turned Melissa down when she asked you for a loan to buy Slater's," her mother continued as if Kate hadn't spoken, "and at first, I thought you were right. But now I wonder. Now I think you're just plain greedy."

Kate was so stunned by her mother's outburst, she simply stood there. Then, in an action she knew she would probably regret, she quietly but firmly pressed Off and ended the call.

CHAPTER 10

The following morning, Kate was still smarting over the argument with her mother and trying to decide if she should call her and apologize when Joanna phoned. Thinking Joanna was going to get on her case about the church building fund, too, Kate's voice was cool.

"I'm calling to invite you to lunch," Joanna said.

"Look, I'm not in the mood for a lecture."

"What are you talking about?"

"Don't tell me Mom didn't call you."

"I haven't talked to Mom except at church yesterday. What's happened?"

Kate sighed. "We had an argument, that's all."

"So what's new?" Joanna said dryly.

"This was kind of serious, and I, um, hung up on her."

"You hung *up* on her!"

"Yes, unfortunately."

"Oh, boy."

Kate sighed.

"So what was the argument about?"

After Kate explained, she said, "What really kills me is Reverend Francis called this my *tithe*. As if I'm *obligated* give him the money."

"Good grief!" Joanna said. "I can't *believe* he actually thinks you should contribute three million dollars! That's pretty nervy. And you know, there are a lot of us who don't even think we *need* a new church. Personally, I think this is an ego trip for him and a couple of the administration committee members."

"Well, the majority voted for it."

"Yeah, but you know how intimidating Clyde Preston and Billie Jamison can be. If they want something, it pretty much gets voted through no matter what the rest of the committee might think."

Kate had heard as much, but hadn't really paid a lot of attention to the gossip since nothing the committee had done in the past had directly affected her.

"So what are you going to do?" Joanna asked.

"I don't know. I guess I'll wait and see what my advisory team says."

"I heard you'd hired some financial experts. Dave was disappointed. He had some ideas for you."

Kate rolled her eyes at the thought of allowing Joanna's husband to give her financial advice. "Yeah, well, so does Mark. And so does Ward McAndrews. But I wanted professionals. *Disinterested* professionals."

"Hey, I don't blame you. I told Dave as much. Anyway, we've gotten way off track. How about lunch today? I was thinking we might drive into Austin, maybe even spend the afternoon shopping."

"Aren't you at work?" Joanna worked as a customer service rep for the local cable company.

"I have a doctor's appointment this morning, so I took the day off."

"Oh. Well, I'd enjoy meeting you for lunch, but I can't be gone the whole day. I have to pick Nicole and Erin up after school."

"What on earth for?"

"Because I don't want them walking home."

"Honestly, Kate, you coddle those kids too much. It won't kill them to walk."

"It's not the walking that's the problem. I'm afraid of someone trying to kidnap them."

"Oh, Lord, I hadn't thought of that. Because of the money, you mean?"

"Yes, because of the money."

"That's awful, Kate."

"Yes, it is."

"Okay, then, let's have lunch somewhere around here. How about that salad place on Fifth Street? The one that just opened last month."

"That sounds good. I've been wanting to try it."

They decided to meet at twelve-thirty. For the rest of the morning, Kate kept busy taking care of all the household chores she'd been neglecting lately. She worked in accompaniment to the sound of constant pounding overhead, because the roofers were still putting on the new roof. At eleven, she headed for the shower and by noon she was ready to go out.

Joanna was already at the restaurant when Kate arrived and had secured a window booth. Kate leaned down to give Joanna a hug, then slid in opposite her.

As always, her sister looked beautifully turned out, in pressed jeans, white tee and fitted pink jacket. Her dark hair, recently colored if the auburn highlights were any indication, had been swept up and secured in the back with a big clip. In Kate's opinion, Joanna looked a good bit younger than her forty-seven years, mainly because she took such good care of herself.

"You look terrific," Kate said.

Joanna made a face. "My butt is spreading, and my thighs are too fat."

"Oh, for heaven's sake. They are not."

"Believe me, they *are*. If I could afford it, I'd have liposuction."

"Joanna, that's ridiculous. There's not an ounce of fat on you."

"You haven't seen me naked." Her green eyes met Kate's. "I'm serious, Kate. I really want to have liposuction."

Kate sighed inwardly. She had a feeling she knew where this was going.

"In fact," Joanna said, "since I know you're planning to do something for each of us, I decided I'd just make it easier for you and give you a list of what I really want."

Kate had thought she was beyond being surprised by anything else, but Joanna had managed to do it. And because she could think of nothing to say that wouldn't cause another argument like the ones she'd had with Mel and her mother, Kate said nothing.

Joanna reached for her purse and took out a folded piece of paper, which she handed to Kate.

Kate opened it. Listed neatly were: a bigger and nicer home, a face-lift, liposuction, a designer wardrobe and a month at the Silver Bell Spa in Santa Fe, New Mexico. She studied the list for a long moment, then finally looked up. "Is this all?"

Joanna grinned. "For starters."

"Is this why you asked me to lunch?"

For the first time, Joanna seemed to realize that Kate might not be thrilled with her list. "Of course not. But I figured since we *were* meeting, why not let you know what I was thinking? I mean, you *are* planning to do something for your family, aren't you?"

"I thought I already *had* done something," Kate said tiredly.

"You won twenty-eight million dollars, Kate. I thought surely you were planning to give each of us more than a car!"

"You know, Joanna, I *was* planning to pay off your mortgage. And I thought I'd establish a college fund for each of the kids. I also thought I might set up trust funds for both you and Mel, something Dave or any other guy you or Mel might hook up with in the future couldn't touch. All totaled, those things would have come to a lot more than these…" She jabbed her finger at the list. "But now I'm wondering if I want to do any of it."

Joanna stared at her. "I can't believe you're mad."

"Let's say I'm hurt. And very disappointed."

"Well, geez, Kate, *excuse* me. I had no idea you'd react like this. I thought I was doing you a favor."

"A favor? Do you know how horrible it is to suddenly have every single person in your life start demanding things? To *expect* them? Then to act as if *you're* the bad guy when you don't immediately say of course you'll do it or you'll buy it? This list is no better than Reverend Francis's demands or Mel's insane idea that I should buy Slater's for *her*."

Just then their waitress came and even though Kate no longer had any appetite for lunch, she ordered the chicken Caesar salad. Joanna ordered Cobb salad with grilled chicken, and finally the waitress left them alone again.

"Mel wants you to buy Slater's?"

"I don't want to talk about it. In fact, I'm not sure I want to talk anymore at all." She reached for her purse, took out two twenty-dollar bills, and placed them on the table. "This should take care of lunch."

Joanna looked stricken when Kate stood up to leave.

"Kate, don't go. Look, I'm *sorry*. I guess I didn't think." Her eyes suddenly filled with tears. "Please," she said more softly. "Please stay."

Kate sighed and sat back down. "I'm sorry, too. I shouldn't have blown up at you like that. But I'm just so tired of everyone wanting a piece of me. You wouldn't believe how many begging letters came in the mail last week. And if I hadn't changed our phone number, I'd have probably needed full-time help to answer the calls."

"You mean, perfect strangers are contacting you?"

Kate nodded.

"Oh, Kate, I had no idea. Is there anything I can do to help? You're not trying to *answer* all the letters, are you?"

"At first I was, but now I'm just tossing them into the trash."

"Which is exactly where they belong."

"Some of the people show up at the house, though. Good thing I hired that security service."

Joanna shook her head. "That's a helluva way to live."

"Tell me about it."

Before Joanna could respond, their waitress approached with their salads. And by the time she'd left and they'd begun eating, Kate didn't want to talk about the money anymore and said so.

"Should I tell you about my loser husband instead?" Joanna asked.

"What's Dave done now?"

"I think he's seeing someone else."

"Oh, Joanna…" Kate knew this wasn't the first time Joanna had suspected Dave of cheating on her. But it was the first time she'd openly admitted it. "Are you sure?"

"Oh, yes. I know all the signs." Joanna stabbed a forkful of salad. "A sudden obsessive interest in his appearance. Too many late nights when he has to work. Keeping his cell phone turned off so I can't call him."

"Have you said anything to him about it?"

Joanna shook her head.

"Why not?" Kate sure would have.

"I don't want a confrontation until I'm ready to kick him out."

"Are you thinking of kicking him out?"

Joanna ate some more of her salad. She shrugged.

"Is this the reason you think you need a face-lift and liposuction?" Kate asked gently.

Joanna's eyes filled with tears and she looked away.

Kate reached across the table and clasped her sister's hand. "I'm so sorry, Joanna. You're worth ten of Dave, you know."

Joanna angrily brushed away her tears. "I don't know why I'm crying over him. I *know* I'm worth ten of him. I just don't know if I have the strength to go it alone, though. I'm forty-seven years *old*, Kate. What man is going to want me now?"

"I don't understand why you think you have to have a man to be happy."

"That's easy for you to say. You're rich."

"I wasn't rich two weeks ago," Kate pointed out.

"And you weren't all that happy, either."

Kate started to say Joanna was wrong, but there was a strong element of truth in what her sister had said. "If I *was* unhappy at times, it was only because it's hard to raise four kids by yourself, especially when money's as tight as it was."

"That proves my point. Money makes a huge difference."

"Okay, I'll give you that. But, Joanna, I'll help you. You know that."

"Will you? You...you're not still mad?"

"No, I'm not mad. Just think things through carefully, okay? And once you've made your decision, we'll go from there."

Kate could tell the moment Nicole got into the car that something was wrong. "Bad day, honey?"

Nicole shrugged and stared out the window.

Erin, too, was unnaturally quiet.

"I wish you girls would talk to me," Kate said. "How can I help if I don't know what's wrong?"

"You *can't* help," Nicole mumbled.

"Try me."

But Nicole remained silent.

So Kate quit trying, figuring she'd wait until later, when Nicole might be more receptive.

Both girls headed for their room as soon as they entered the house. Kate was grateful to see the roofers were finished. In fact, most of the crew had gone. Only the foreman—a young man named Brett Kubrick—and a couple of men were left, and they were cleaning up.

The foreman knocked at the back door a few minutes later. "Just wanted to let you know we're done, Ms. Bishop. Mr. Wayland'll be sendin' you a final bill."

"Okay, good."

"You wanna take a look? See if everything looks all right?"

"Oh, I'm sure it's fine. I know Wayland's does a great job." She smiled. "Besides, if everything *isn't* fine, I won't pay the rest of what I owe."

He smiled, too, his blue eyes twinkling.

Kate waited, thinking he would say goodbye and leave, but still he stood there. She began to feel a bit uncomfortable. What did he want?

"Uh, I was wondering," he said, "you ever gone line dancing?"

Kate blinked. "Me? Line dancing?"

He smiled again. "Yeah. Line dancing. It's a lot of fun. Me and some of my friends, we go to Jimmy's, out on the old Kickapoo Highway, on Friday nights. They have a great band, great beer, great dancing. Thought maybe you'd like to go with me one of these nights."

Kate was flabbergasted. For a moment, she couldn't

think how to answer. Why, Brett Kubrick couldn't be more than twenty-five years old! She was old enough to be his *mother*. "Um, I appreciate the invitation," she finally said, "but I'm a little old for that kind of thing."

"You don't look very old to me."

"Mr. Kubrick, I have nineteen-year-old twins."

"Call me Brett." He seemed unfazed by her statement. "And so what? I have a nineteen-year-old brother. So we've got somethin' in common."

Kate couldn't help it; she laughed. "I'm really flattered, Brett, but I'm way too old for you."

"Why don't you let me decide that?"

Kate smiled and shook her head. "Thanks again, but no thanks."

After he'd finally gone, the smile remained on her face. Maybe the money she'd won had influenced his invitation, but for some reason, she didn't think so. His interest had been genuine. You couldn't fake that kind of thing. Or was she kidding herself because that's what she *wanted* to believe? Oh, who cared? It was fun to be asked out by a young, good-looking boy. And even if it wasn't true, it was fun to think she was still attractive enough and sexy enough to interest him.

Frankly, she was sick of thinking about the money. Of believing every good thing that had happened to her in the past couple of weeks had to be related to the lottery. Because the truth was, if she *really* believed that, she wasn't sure she'd even want to keep her winnings.

* * *

"So what did Lucy have to say when you told her you wanted to break up?" This was the first chance Tessa'd had to ask Tom about Lucy, because he was asleep when she got home from work, or out, or there were too many people around or something.

"Uh…"

"What?"

He made a face.

"Tom! You haven't told her yet, have you?"

Sheepishly, he shook his head.

"Why *not*?"

"Oh, hell, Tessa, I don't know. Every time I start to, I can't seem to get it out. It's like she knows what I'm gonna say and somehow we end up…you know…and then how can I tell her?"

"Tom."

"I know, I know."

He pushed his hands through his hair in a gesture Tessa recognized meant he was frustrated.

"The longer you wait, the worse it'll get."

"I know."

He looked so unhappy, she just wanted to put her arms around him and tell him it would be okay. But they weren't kids anymore. They were nineteen. Old enough to serve in the military and go to war. Old enough to vote.

"You…you always use a condom, don't you?" She'd

lowered her voice automatically, although no one else was at home.

"Geez, Tess, do you think I'm *stupid?* Lucy's on the Pill, anyway."

"That's good." She bit her lip. Lucy was an only child. Her parents were divorced, and her mother—a neonatal nurse—worked the four to midnight shift at the local hospital, so it was easy for Lucy and Tom to be alone.

"Quit worrying, okay? I'm gonna tell her. But you know, she's kind of emotional."

Tessa just shook her head. "Tom, you're just too nice. That's why you seem to attract these clingy, needy types."

He shrugged dejectedly. "I never know they're clingy and needy when we start out."

Tessa sighed. "Yeah. I know."

"Besides, I *do* like her."

"Well, you have to do this your way, but I really think you're making a big mistake dragging this out. It's just going to get harder and harder to tell her. Just make up your mind, and do it." His pained look made her hurt for him. "Do you want *me* to do it for you?"

His head jerked around. "No! Geez, Tess, I'm not *that* big a jerk. I'll do it. I just have to pick the right time."

"You're not a jerk at all." She reached across his bed where they both sat with their backs against the headboard and squeezed his hand. "I love you. You know that, don't you?"

He smiled, although the smile was strained. "Yeah. Me, too."

Tessa laughed. "Oh, I *know* you love yourself. After all, you're a guy."

She was still laughing as she escaped through the door only seconds before he threw a pillow at her.

CHAPTER 11

Erin stuffed her books into her backpack, took her purse and jacket out of her locker, then hoisted everything into her arms and walked outside, heading for the school pickup area in the front turnaround.

When she got there, she looked over the line of cars but didn't see her mom's Lexus. Sighing—she was hungry and she had a ton of homework—she dropped her backpack on the ground and sat on it.

"Hey, Erin, you going to the game tomorrow night?"

The questioner was Rachel Ferris, one of Erin's friends.

"Don't know yet. Prob'ly," Erin said. At least, she *hoped* she was. Her mom had gotten so weird lately and didn't seem to want Erin to go anywhere. Erin frowned. It was all because of that money. Sometimes Erin wished her mother hadn't even won the lottery.

Marcy waved goodbye. "See you tomorrow." She headed for the bike rack and, minutes later, disappeared down the drive and into the street.

Erin sighed again. She liked riding her bike to and

from school, but her mother wouldn't allow her to do that anymore, either. Getting picked up by your mother was for babies.

"Hey, Erin!"

Erin looked around and saw Heidi. She grinned and waved.

When Heidi got closer she said, "You want a ride? My mom's here today."

"Can't. My mom's coming and she won't know where I am."

"Call her."

"Oh. Yeah." Sometimes Erin forgot they all had cell phones now. Whipping hers out of the front pocket of her pack, she flipped it open and pressed three.

"You've reached Kate Bishop. Please leave a message."

Damn. Erin knew her mother would have a fit if she knew Erin sometimes thought the word *damn*, but she hated when she got Kate's voice mail. Why have cell phones if you weren't going to answer? Scowling, she closed the phone. "She's not answering," she told Heidi.

"So? Leave her a message."

"What if she doesn't get it and comes and waits? She'll be mad."

"Yeah." Heidi nodded glumly. They both knew how unreasonable parents could be. "Call me when you get home, okay?"

"Okay."

Ten minutes later, most of the cars that had been waiting when Erin came outside were gone and Erin was still sitting there with no sign of her mom's Lexus. Taking her cell phone out, she tried calling Kate again, and once more got her voice mail. This time, she did leave a message, saying, "Mom? Where *are* you? Almost everyone's gone! I've been waiting at least twenty minutes."

Snapping the phone closed, she stood, picked up the backpack and the rest of her stuff, and decided to walk out to the street to see if she could spy her mother coming.

Nearing the end of the driveway, she heard a pitiful mewling sound coming from the direction of the boxwoods lining the edge of the school's property. She stopped, frowning. Then she heard it again.

"Kitty?" she called softly, walking toward the shrubbery. "Where are you?"

A moment later she saw the cat—a bony gray with short fur shivering under the hedge. "Oh, poor kitty," she crooned. "Are you cold?" Kneeling down, she reached in to pet it, but the cat—maybe used to being mistreated—backed away from her hand. When Erin got down on her hands and knees and tried to coax the cat forward, it just backed up farther.

Erin could see the cat was just skin and bones. She wondered if her mom would let her keep it if she could get it to come out. Prob'ly not. She remembered when their neighbor's cat had had a litter and Erin had wanted to keep one of the babies. Her mom had said then that they had enough pets to feed and take care of. They didn't need another. But maybe now that they were rich, her mom wouldn't care *how* many animals they had, as long as Erin promised to take care of it. First, though, Erin had to get the cat to come out.

Erin sat back on her heels and tried to think how to accomplish this. Then she remembered she hadn't eaten everything in her lunch. In fact, she had a piece of cheese in her backpack.

Reaching for it, she nearly shrieked when someone grabbed her shoulders. Thinking it was her mom, she turned around to see a dark-eyed man she didn't recognize.

"What are you doing?" she cried, trying to pull away. "Let me go!"

But he didn't let go. Instead, he tightened his grip and began dragging her away from the bushes.

Erin was so shocked, it was a moment before she reacted and began to kick and scream.

But he was a lot bigger and stronger than she was, and her pitiful efforts didn't deter him. He simply clapped one hand over her mouth and with the other, reached to open a car door.

Terrified, Erin fought as hard as she could, because she knew if he managed to put her in that car, she might never see her mother or anyone else again.

* * *

"Damn!" Kate said, pushing down on the gas pedal. She couldn't believe she'd forgotten her cell phone and so hadn't been able to call Erin to tell her she was running late. Oh, she was so mad at herself.

She breathed a sigh of relief as she finally turned onto the street where Erin's school was located. She was only sixteen minutes late. That wasn't too bad. Erin would be upset, but Kate was certain she'd still be there. She was too responsible not to be.

More responsible than I am.

She slowed down as she approached the school and was just about to turn right into the circular driveway when, out of the corner of her eye, she saw something that didn't look right. Two people struggling. No, a man and a *child* struggling.

Omigod, that's Erin!

Kate's heart slammed into her throat. Wrenching the steering wheel to the left, she hit the accelerator and shot over the curb, bouncing onto the street. Then, in a reflexive act she would later second-guess, she rammed her car into the back of the dark sedan where a man was struggling to put her daughter.

Screaming, "Stop! Stop!" Kate leaped out of the car.

"Mom!" Erin screamed. She scrambled off the grass where she'd landed when the Lexus had hit the dark sedan and ran toward Kate.

The man—whom Kate did not recognize—ran

around to the driver's side of his car and jumped in. Seconds later, he was gone, but not before Kate had seen and memorized his license plate.

Holding Erin, Kate was shaking so violently, she could hardly talk.

"Mom, he tried to kidnap me!" Erin sobbed in Kate's arms.

All Kate could think was, what if she had been a couple of minutes later? Erin would have been gone. Her baby would have been gone.

Later, in describing the incident to the police, Kate managed to calm down enough to give them a description of the man and his car, as well as the license number.

"You're one lucky kid," the officer said. "Your mother did the right thing."

"This was all my fault," Kate corrected. "I was late. I should have been here fifteen minutes earlier."

"Hey, it happens," the officer said. "Don't beat up on yourself."

But Kate knew she would, because it *was* her fault that Erin had been frightened out of her mind and almost kidnapped by who knows *what* kind of pervert.

"Oh, Kate," Linda said later when Kate called her. "How scary! God, what's *wrong* with people? No one is safe anymore."

"It's all because of the money," Kate said wearily. The kids were finally all home and safe in their beds, but every time she thought about what the outcome of today's incident could have been, she started trembling again.

"You don't know that. He could have been just waiting for the first girl he saw."

"That does it. I'm moving the girls to St. Christine's," Kate said, naming an exclusive all-girls private school thirty miles north of Cranbrook. "Their security is top-notch."

"Have you told them yet?"

"No. I'll tell them tomorrow."

"They're not going to be happy."

"I'd rather have them unhappy for a while than killed or held for ransom." Just the thought made her sick to her stomach.

"You know, Kate, changing their school might not be the best answer to your problem."

"What do you mean?"

"Well, even going to a new school, they still have to get there and back. That's the vulnerable time, right?"

"Right," Kate said thoughtfully.

"Seems to me you should concentrate on finding a way to transport them that doesn't depend on you exclusively. And," Linda added, "I'd seriously consider moving to a more secure house. Maybe in one of those new, gated communities. Frankly, I think *all* of you need a safer environment, not just the kids. Shoot,

Kate, some nut could hide out behind your garage and grab you when you go out to get in the car!"

"I know, but—"

"No buts. You need to get out of there. All of you. And if you don't have your phone listed, none of these nuts will know where you've gone."

"But if we move, Erin would still have to change schools."

"She'll have to go to a new school in the fall, anyway, won't she?"

"Yes, but all her friends will be going with her."

"Well, think about what I've said."

Kate did think about it. In fact, she slept little that night for stewing over the problem. The following morning, she told the kids they were going to have a family meeting that evening.

"I'll order pizza or Chinese, whichever you want, and we'll hash out this problem. In the meantime…" Here she looked at Nicole and Erin in particular. "Do not, under any circumstances, leave the pickup area at your school, no matter *what*."

"Okay."

"I mean it, Erin. Let yesterday be a lesson to you. That man could not have grabbed you like that if you hadn't been so close to the street. I'm not saying it's your fault," she added, seeing the tears spring to Erin's eyes, "but he wouldn't have had the opportunity if you'd stayed in the pickup area."

"But you were so late, Mom…"

"I know that, honey. I shouldn't have been late, and I should have paid attention when I changed purses and made sure I had my cell phone with me. What happened yesterday was my fault, and I take full responsibility. But still, let's not make it easier for some crazy person to get his hands on you."

For a while, the five of them discussed the money and how tempting it was for someone unscrupulous or desperate to view it as the answer to their problems and from there to decide to kidnap one of them and hold them for ransom.

They were in the middle of this discussion when the phone rang. It was Scott Logan, the chief of police, calling to inform Kate that they'd caught the man who had tried to abduct Erin yesterday.

"Oh, thank God," Kate said.

"Turns out he lost his job a couple of months ago, and the bank is foreclosing on his house. Guess he was desperate and couldn't think of a way out. He's got a coupla kids of his own."

"Well, I'm sorry for his troubles, but that doesn't make it all right for him to do what he did."

"No, 'course it doesn't, and I didn't mean to imply it did. Just wanted you to know he wasn't some pervert. I really don't think he'd have hurt Erin."

"What's going to happen to him now?"

"He's in custody here at the jail. He'll have to appear

in court tomorrow and the judge'll either set bail or not, depending. If his case goes to trial, you and Erin might have to testify."

"I hope it doesn't come to that." Kate hated the thought of Erin having to appear in court.

"He might just plead guilty and throw himself upon the mercy of the court."

They talked a while longer, then Kate said, "Thank you for letting me know."

"Uh, Kate…"

"Yes?"

"I think you should take some precautions from now on."

"I plan to."

"Good. You need our help, we'll be glad to help out."

After taking the girls to school, Kate headed to the dentist's office. She was scheduled for a routine cleaning, but she also needed to talk to her dentist about the root canal he thought she needed. After examining it and giving her his recommendation, he sat back and smiled down at her.

"I heard about your big win."

"Hasn't everyone?" Kate said wryly.

"Cranbrook's a small town. That kind of news travels fast."

They chatted awhile. Then, catching her off guard,

he said, "I was wondering…would you like to have dinner with me some night?"

"I, uh…" She frowned. "Aren't you *married*, Dr. Dickson?"

He grimaced. "Was married. Marleen and I were divorced six months ago."

"Oh."

"So what do you think?"

"Um, I don't know." Kate's mind raced. "Um, right now things are pretty crazy. I'm thinking of moving."

"Away from Cranbrook?"

"Maybe. I haven't decided yet." Kate was fudging the truth, but she didn't care. She didn't trust any of these men who were asking her out now. They'd certainly never shown any interest in her before.

"Well, we'd sure hate to see you go." He squeezed her arm. "I've always liked you, Kate. But I was never free to say so before. So if you change your mind…"

Kate breathed a huge sigh of relief when he finally left the examining room. For the rest of the day, she thought about how her lottery win was a mixed blessing. From becoming a whole lot more popular with the opposite sex to becoming a whole lot more *unpopular* with her family because she wasn't doing what they wanted her to, the money had turned her world upside down.

And now…she had to decide whether or not to sell the house and move.

That night, over pizza and salad, she talked to the kids about it.

"I won't have to change schools if we move, will I?" Nicole said.

"No. Not if we stay in Cranbrook."

"What about me?" Erin said.

"I think you can probably stay at your school for the rest of the year."

"What about next year?"

"You'll probably be going to a different middle school then. It really depends on where we find a house." But Kate knew that none of the newer, gated communities were in their section of town.

"I want to go to Hawkins with Heidi and my friends," Erin said, tears already forming.

"Don't be such a baby," Nicole said.

"Nicole," Kate warned, "if you were the one facing going to a different school than your friends, you'd be upset, too."

"I wouldn't be *crying*."

"Why are you being so mean to her?" Tom said, getting up and going over to Erin. Kneeling by her, he said, "Hey, it won't be so bad. You'll make new friends. And Heidi will still be your friend."

"I wish nothing had to change," Erin sobbed. "Why does everything have to *change?*"

"But some of the changes are good," Tessa said. "Aren't they?"

"Yeah, well, of course *you'd* think so," Nicole said. "You and Tom got new cars. All I've gotten is a bunch of my so-called friends wanting me to pay for everything when we go places."

Kate stared at her. "Why didn't you tell me this was going on, honey?"

"What could *you* do about it?" Nicole said.

Before Kate could answer, Tessa said, "I've had the same thing happen, Mom. Only my friends have wanted to borrow money from me." She smiled cynically. "They don't really want to borrow anything. They want me to give it to them."

"Yeah!" Nicole said. "Tracy wanted me to give her two hundred dollars so she could buy a dress for the spring dance."

Kate was shocked. Although why she should be, she didn't know. After all, everyone *she* knew wanted money from her, too. Why should the kids' friends be any different? "What about you, Tom? Has this kind of thing happened to you, too?"

He nodded glumly. "Not so much with my friends, but a couple of the guys at work have hit me up for a loan."

"Did you *give* them money?"

He made a face. "Not a lot. Just a twenty here or there."

"Tom."

"I know, Mom, but geez, it's hard to say no."

"Tom," Kate said, "you're too nice."

"Yeah, I hear that a lot."

Kate wondered about the odd note in his voice, but she was too upset over this money business to pursue it. "That settles it," she said. "We're moving. Maybe *all* of you need new friends. And you know what? I think you and Tessa should quit those jobs, Tom. There's no reason you have to keep working now."

Tom frowned. "I don't want to quit. In fact, I wanted to talk to you about something. I was just waiting until—" He broke off. "Now's not the time, though. We can talk about it later."

"Is something wrong?" Kate asked.

"No. It's just I've been rethinking going to flight school."

"Oh?"

"Yeah, but let's talk about it later, okay?"

Kate realized he didn't want to discuss his future in front of everyone else, so she said okay.

Later, when Tom had gone out and the girls were busy with homework and the house was quiet, Kate decided to call Mark. She wanted to tell him about putting the house on the market before one of the kids did.

"I'm not surprised," he said. "I figured you'd want something nicer now that you're rich."

Telling herself not to get irritated, she said, "That's not the reason we're going to move."

"Yeah, well, whatever…"

"You know, Mark, I expected you, of all people, to understand. Surely you want your kids to be safe."

"How's you moving going to prevent some nutso from trying to kidnap one of the kids again?"

"Those new gated communities have full-time security patrols."

"What about getting them to and from school?"

"I'm thinking of hiring a bodyguard to drive Erin and Nicole back and forth."

"Christ," Mark said. "This is crazy!"

"I know, but what else can I do? Anyway, I wanted you to know, and I also wanted to tell you that when we do sell the house, you'll get whatever we clear on it."

"Oh. Okay."

Kate frowned. He certainly didn't seem very excited. Or even very pleased. "It will probably be close to fifty thousand."

"That's all?"

Kate's mouth dropped open. "You sound disappointed," she finally said.

"Yeah, well, maybe I am."

"What's *wrong* with you, Mark? If I'd told you a couple of months ago that I was going to give you fifty thousand dollars, you'd have been dancing on the ceiling."

It was a moment before he answered. "You really don't know what's wrong?"

"Why don't you spell it out for me?"

"Well, hell, Kate, you've got twenty-eight *million* dollars, yet you expect me to be thrilled about a measly fifty *thousand?* I mean, **can** you spare it?"

"You know, Mark, I shouldn't have to point out to you that we are no longer married, *and* that I don't owe you a damned thing."

"I know you don't *owe* me anything, Kate, but I guess I naively thought you might *want* to do something nice for me."

"And a gift of fifty thousand dollars as well as a brand-new truck *isn't* nice?"

When he didn't answer, she said, "Frankly, I cannot believe that you really expect me to give you a share of my winnings."

"I guess I shouldn't be surprised that you don't intend to," he said bitterly. "After all, you always *did* think only of yourself."

His accusation was so unfair and so untrue, Kate was stunned into silence. For a moment, she simply stared at the phone. Then for the second time in a week, she pressed the Off button and disconnected the call.

Immediately, she regretted her impulsive act, because since their divorce, she had bent over backwards trying to keep their relationship cordial and cooperative, for the kids' sake, if no other. But there *was* another reason. There were *two* other reasons—Mark's parents—with whom Kate had continued to have a warm, even loving, relationship.

She didn't want that to change. She knew she would somehow have to try to patch things up with Mark, even if it meant giving him more money. The thought galled her, yet the alternative seemed worse.

Why did money seem to bring out the worst in people? she wondered as she prepared for bed. In her wildest dreams, she'd never have believed that her family and friends would act the way they had since she'd won the lottery. It was as if all good sense had flown out the window and pure greed had taken over.

Her last thought before falling asleep was that if things didn't get better soon, she might just say the hell with everyone and give all the money to charity.

CHAPTER 12

Harriet August was fit to be tied. She couldn't believe Kate was being so stubborn! She was acting as if giving the church three million dollars was going to put her in a homeless shelter or something, even though she had more money than she could spend in five lifetimes.

She still couldn't get over that Kate had hung up on her. Oh, she'd apologized, even though it had taken her three days to call back and do so, but since then, no matter what Harriet said, Kate hadn't changed her mind. She'd insisted on being given the blueprints for the proposed new church, as well as any contracts the administrative council had already signed so that her "financial team," as she called it, could look everything over and decide if it was a smart investment for her.

Smart investment!

How ridiculous could a person be? Of course it was a smart investment. Any time a person gave to the Lord for the Lord's work, the investment was smart. Kate had certainly strayed far from her roots if she no longer thought so. If money was more important to her than her faith and her church.

Where did I go wrong with my girls? Why are they all so different from what I hoped they'd be?

But, as always, there was no answer to Harriet's question. She only knew she'd done the best she could under less-than-ideal circumstances. She'd worked hard, she'd sacrificed, she'd stressed living a good life, going to church, believing in God, accepting responsibility for yourself and the value of a good education.

And now here she was, with one daughter miserably unhappy in her marriage and with the mistaken notion that spending money on expensive clothes and jewelry would make up for all her disappointments; another daughter who couldn't seem to hold a job or keep her daughter in line and, Harriet was sorely afraid, was sexually reckless; and now Kate…who had turned out to be the biggest disappointment of all. And not a single one of them had finished college or had a career they could be proud of.

Why, God? What have I done to deserve this?

But there was no answer to that question, either.

Harriet blinked back tears.

Some days she wished she'd never had any children. Life would certainly be easier. But then she thought about her grandchildren. Granted, Joanna's three all seemed to have problems, as did Melissa's Leeann, but Harriet had to admit that Kate's children were turning out very well. They were all ambitious and smart, and none of them had ever given Kate or Mark any trouble.

Harriet's two favorites were Tom and Erin—Tom because he was her only grandson and a fine young man. And Erin… Harriet smiled tenderly, thinking of Erin. From the day Erin was born, Harriet had felt a special closeness to her, and she knew Erin felt the same way, for Erin had confessed her feelings once.

"Gran," she'd said, "you're my bestest grandma."

"Better than your Grandma Bishop?" Harriet had said, even as she knew she shouldn't encourage Erin to make comparisons.

"Lots better," Erin said solemnly. She'd been four at the time, but she'd been solemn from birth. An "old soul" someone had once said, and Harriet agreed. It was one of things she loved most about Erin.

Harriet had smiled and hugged her then, saying, "And I think you're the best, too."

Erin had been too young to respond by trying to pin Harriet down or make her admit that she loved Erin more than her other granddaughters, but Harriet knew the child had felt her love and, ever since, they'd had a bond between them than was unshakable.

Maybe Erin would fulfill all the dreams Harriet had once had for her own daughters.

If that happened, everything Harriet had endured over the years—all the hardships, all the sacrifices, all the heartache—would be worthwhile.

* * *

It took Tom until the first of April to break up with Lucy. They were sitting in the living room of her mom's house. As usual, her mom was at work. Lucy had just popped some popcorn and they were going to watch a new movie from a service she subscribed to. It was one of those romantic chick flicks. Tom didn't have much interest in watching it, but lately he'd given in to just about anything Lucy wanted to do because he knew he couldn't wait any longer to break things off. Things had reached a point between them where he could hardly stand to be around her anymore, because he couldn't talk about anything related to his future plans without her getting teary-eyed.

Unknowingly, she gave him the perfect opening.

"Jason and Maddie broke up," she said as she took the DVD out of its wrapper.

"Doesn't surprise me," Tom said.

"Well, it surprised *Maddie*," Lucy said.

"It shouldn't have. The last couple of times we were around them, I could see Jase wanted out."

"You're just saying that."

"Why would I say it if it wasn't true?"

"Because guys always stick together."

Tom snorted. "And girls *don't?*"

"Well, if he wanted out, he should have *told* Maddie instead of skulking around. She found out he's been seeing Natalie Delinsky behind her back. *Screwing* Natalie Delinsky," she added scornfully.

"You're right," Tom said slowly. "He shouldn't have done that."

"No, he *shouldn't*," Lucy said.

"But maybe he was desperate."

She stopped in the act of inserting the DVD into the player and looked at him. "What do you mean?"

"I mean it's hard to tell someone you don't want to see them anymore." Tom took a deep breath. His heart gave a painful knock. *Do it now.* "I know how he must have felt."

Their eyes met. For a long moment, the only sound in the room was the shallow breathing of her mother's ancient golden retriever. Slowly, two bright spots of color stained Lucy's cheeks. She shook her head wordlessly.

"Luce…"

"No," she whispered.

"Luce, I'm sorry. I—I just need some space." *Don't lie to her….* "No, that's not true. I—I want to be free. I don't want to be tied down to anyone." Seeing the tears that had sprung into her eyes, he said hurriedly, before he lost his nerve, "The thing is, you want to get married. And I don't. I probably won't get married until I'm at least ten years older than I am now."

She put the DVD down and began to cry. Walking over, she reached for him, saying, "You don't mean that, Tom. You love me. I know you do."

Tom hardened his heart and stood, evading her touch. "I can't do this anymore, Luce. I've felt this way for a while, but I didn't want to hurt you, so I didn't say anything. But that's cheating every bit as much as Jason was cheating on Maddie."

She threw herself at him, wrapping her arms around him and sobbing against his chest. "I—I can't live without you, Tom. I love you so much. Please don't leave me. Please. I-I'll be anything you want. I won't get in your way, I promise. I love you. I love you."

"Lucy, don't do this…"

"I can't live without you. I can't." She was crying so hard now, her whole body was shaking. "I'll kill myself if you leave me."

Jesus, how had he gotten himself into this? What the hell was he going to do now? What if she was serious? He almost said he hadn't meant it, but then, suddenly, from somewhere, he remembered something he'd read once—one of those advice columns for teens that the paper occasionally carried. The therapist who wrote the column had said teens are especially vulnerable to emotional blackmail, but each person needed to learn that they were not responsible for someone else's happiness or choices.

Gripping Lucy's arms firmly, Tom loosened her hold and backed away from her. "I can't stop you from doing anything you want to do," he said. "The truth is, I don't love you the way you say you love me. And I can't pretend to feel that way when I don't. It's not fair to you, and it's not fair to me."

He was two feet from the front door when the book struck his head.

"I hate you," she shrieked. "I hate you!"

He could still hear her screaming at him after he shut the door behind him.

By the middle of April, Kate's house had sold and she'd found another she liked. The new one was located in Shadow Hills, about eight miles northeast of the Cranbrook city limits, although the children living there attended Cranbrook schools. The enclave had two entrances, both gated, with a twenty-four-hour guard at each gate and a twenty-four-hour security patrol around the grounds, all of which was enclosed by an eight-foot-high brick wall.

The brick wall wouldn't keep out someone determined to get in, but it was definitely a deterrent. The home Kate had selected was in the middle of the complex. It was less than a year old, two stories, built of a soft, fawn-colored brick with black shutters. It had a pool with a spa, a three-car garage and a screened-in Florida room overlooking the backyard. The property was also completely fenced in for privacy, and added security.

"What do you think?" she asked the kids, for she'd never buy a house without consulting them. Especially now, when everyone seemed right on the edge most of the time.

When the kids agreed, Kate gave her Realtor the go-ahead.

One of things that had sold the kids was that for the first time, they would each have a room of their own. Tom and Tessa even had private baths. Nicole and Erin had to share a bath, but they didn't mind at all, because as soon as Tessa left for school, Nicole would have her bathroom to use.

Kate, in an effort to take some of the sting from the move away from friends and familiar things, told the kids they were going to give away all of their old furniture and could furnish their bedrooms any way they pleased. She even said she'd hire someone to paint the walls the colors of their choice. She crossed her fingers, hoping no one would want black or something else horrible, but they chose beautiful colors.

Tom wanted dark blue and picked heavy, masculine furniture with blue-and-green-striped bedding. Tessa went feminine, choosing violet walls, white French provincial furniture and lovely blue and lavender florals to go with it. Nicole picked a deep salmon shade for her walls and light contemporary furniture. And Erin selected a gorgeous sea green and warm, honeyed woods.

Kate was proud of them. They all had good taste.

Kate, too, allowed herself the luxury of new furniture and here she really indulged herself. She went with dark woods, pale turquoise walls and brown, turquoise and peach for her bedding and accents. She visited a highly touted art gallery in Austin and, after careful study and consultation with a decorator, bought two beautiful paintings to hang where she'd see them first thing upon awakening in the mornings.

The same decorator helped her furnish the rest of the house and Kate had to admit she loved everything. It was very nice to have no limits on what you could spend. Very nice to have a home you were proud to show off.

Several times during this two-month period before they moved into the new house, Adam Marino called her to invite her to dinner or a movie. She accepted twice, and both times she enjoyed herself tremendously. Each time, he kissed her good-night, but didn't press her for more. For this, she was profoundly grateful, even as she was a bit disappointed. She couldn't help wondering if, for some reason, he no longer found her desirable. But then why did he continue to ask her out?

If only her family wasn't so unhappy with her, she might have been happy herself. Although Kate had apologized to her mother, Harriet was still cool. Of course, if Kate had decided to give her pastor the three million he wanted, she would have easily gotten back into her mother's good graces. But her team of three— Adam, Keith and the accountant—had strongly advised against it.

"The church's income doesn't support this kind of investment," Keith said. "And the size of the congregation doesn't warrant a bigger church. My feeling is there's ego involved here."

That's what Kate had thought. But when she'd attempted to explain her decision to her mother, her mother didn't even try to disguise her disappointment and disapproval.

And then there were her sisters. Joanna had decided not to confront Dave, at least not yet. Kate understood that it was her decision, but she refused to give Joanna any large sums of money until her personal life was more settled. What Kate suspected, although she didn't say this to Joanna, was that if she gave Joanna a couple of million dollars, Dave would then leave her, secure in the knowledge that, under Texas law, he would be entitled to half. Kate didn't want to be the catalyst in the breakup of her sister's marriage. If they were to split, it had to be Joanna's decision.

And Mel...Mel wouldn't talk to Kate. Slater's had sold to someone else, and Mel couldn't forgive Kate for not backing her. The fact that her financial team had strongly advised against doing so meant nothing to Mel. They were sisters. If Kate loved her, Kate would have bought Slater's for her. Nothing Kate said made any difference. Kate knew the only way Mel would forget about Slater's was if Kate were to give her a big chunk of money.

They all wanted money!

All of them.

And Mark was still giving her the cold shoulder, even though he was getting nearly sixty thousand out of the sale of the old house, much more than she'd originally thought. And he'd gotten the new truck and no longer had to make a five-hundred-dollar child support payment each month. You'd think he'd be satisfied. Even grateful. But no, he wanted more. It made her so mad every time she thought about it, she wanted to scream.

At least he hadn't turned his parents against her. The elder Bishops were still as warm and loving as they'd always been when Kate saw them, and she knew they were genuinely happy for her.

Maybe they are the only ones who are.

But no, Linda was happy for her, too.

Thank God for Linda. What Kate would do without her, she didn't know. Hopefully, she'd never have to find out.

The excitement over the new house wore off quickly, especially once the younger girls realized how hard it was going to be to see their old friends. They lived too far away for easy visiting back and forth and had to depend on Kate or the twins to take them everywhere. That had been true at the old house, too—especially after Kate won the lottery—but there was a big difference between driving them somewhere that was only five minutes away and driving them somewhere that took thirty minutes.

"It's no fun living here if none of my friends can come over," Nicole complained after they'd been in the house three weeks.

"I'll be happy to go and pick them up," Kate said, even though she was sick of playing chauffeur. She often thought longingly of the days when Nicole and Erin could hop on their bikes and pretty much go anywhere they wanted.

"Nothing is any fun anymore," Erin grumbled. "I don't like it here."

"But this house has everything we've ever dreamed of," Kate said, even though she missed their old neighborhood, too. "I thought you loved your beautiful new bedrooms and the pool. Don't you love the pool?"

Erin shrugged. "I don't like swimming by myself."

Kate sighed. "School will be out soon, honey. Then you can have Heidi and Rachel and anyone else you like come and stay and you'll have lots of friends to swim with."

"If they want to," Erin said.

"What do you mean, *if they want to?* Of course they'll want to."

Erin frowned.

Kate put down the knife she'd been using to cut up celery in preparation for making tuna salad for tomorrow's lunches. She walked over to where Erin was sitting at the kitchen table doing her homework. "Honey, what is it? What did you mean by that?"

Erin looked away, but not before Kate saw a tear roll down her cheek.

"Please tell me what's wrong," Kate said softly. She knelt by Erin.

"Heidi's been hanging out with that new girl. The one who moved from San Antonio. Liliana."

"Well, you like Liliana, too, don't you?"

"I *did*."

"You mean you don't anymore?"

Erin bit her lip. She refused to look at Kate.

"Erin?"

"I hate her," she finally said vehemently.

"Erin. You don't hate anybody."

"Yes, I do!" Erin glared at her. "She sucks."

"Erin! Don't say that word. It's disgusting."

"Well, she does."

"What did Liliana do to you to make you say such a thing?"

"She told Heidi I smell funny. She said I was stupid, that I like animals more than people. She said nobody really likes me, and if Heidi did, she was stupid, too. I *hate* her!" At that, Erin burst into tears, threw down her pencil, jumped up from the table and ran out of the room.

Kate heard her thundering up the stairs and, a few seconds later, the slam of her bedroom door. Kate sank down on the chair Erin had vacated. Her heart was pounding as if she was the one who'd raced upstairs and not Erin.

My life is spinning out of control.

Kate had never felt so helpless. Even in those dark days after the decision to divorce Mark, she'd never felt quite so lost and uncertain.

She sat there for a long time. The house was very quiet. If Erin was crying upstairs, she was doing it silently. The twins were out—Tom at a basketball game and Tessa in Austin, spending the night with a high school friend. And Nicole was babysitting for Mark and Heather and would be spending the night there.

Kate finally heaved a sigh and got wearily to her feet. She'd finish making the tuna salad and then go up and check on Erin. She'd just finished mixing in the mayonnaise when the phone rang.

"Hello?" At the same time she heard Erin say hello upstairs.

"Kate?" It was Linda.

Kate heard the click that said Erin had hung up. "Hi, Linda."

"What's wrong?"

Kate smiled wryly. "How'd you know something was wrong?"

"Your voice is a dead giveaway."

"What *isn't* wrong?" Geez, she sounded sorry for herself.

"Said the woman with twenty-eight million dollars."

"I know. I should be jumping for joy every single day."

"Yes, you should. Now, seriously, what *is* wrong?"

"Let's see…well, number one, Tom's been acting

weird for weeks, but when I ask him what's wrong, he says nothing and not to worry about it."

"I hate when kids say that. It usually makes all my antennae start to hum."

"I know." Kate really *was* worried about Tom. He'd never been moody like the girls, yet lately he always seemed to have his mind somewhere else. Even the excitement of being accepted by two of the universities he'd applied to hadn't seemed to banish whatever it was that was troubling him.

"So is that it?" Linda said. "'Cause that just seems kind of normal."

"That's just the beginning. Added to that, my entire family hates me. And tonight Erin had a meltdown."

"Erin? Why?"

"Apparently no one likes her anymore, including Heidi, her former best friend."

"God, I wouldn't want to be a teenager again for anything."

"Me, either."

"So why don't the kids like her anymore?"

"Who knows? Kids are a total mystery to me."

Linda laughed. "If they're a mystery to you, kiddo, the rest of us don't stand a chance."

After a moment, Kate laughed, too, and it felt good. She was so tired of turmoil and arguments and people being mad at her.

"Tell Erin her Aunt Linda wants to take her to San

Antonio on Saturday. We'll go shopping, have lunch on the river and see a movie. Maybe that'll cheer her up."

"That would cheer *me* up."

"Well, you come, too. We can even stay overnight. Just have a blast, the three of us. Unless you think Nicole would enjoy coming with us."

"I don't know what Nicole would enjoy anymore. I told you. The kids are a mystery to me."

"So you said."

"But I'll ask her. And yes, I think going away for the weekend is a fabulous idea." But Kate was already worrying about leaving the twins on their own, even though she knew it was ridiculous. They would be on their own soon enough, and they *were* nineteen. So what if Tom seemed preoccupied? After all, *he* was technically still a teenager himself.

Nicole wasn't interested in going to San Antonio for the weekend. "Mother," she said in exasperation the following day, "you know I have the spring concert Saturday night."

Kate had forgotten. Oh, God, she was turning into a terrible mother. No wonder the kids were unhappy. "I'm sorry. I forgot."

"You always forget the things *I'm* doing." So saying, Nicole stormed off to her room.

Kate's eyes filled with tears. What was *wrong* with her? What was wrong with *all* of them?

"Nothing is wrong with you, Kate," Linda said when Kate called her to tell her what had happened. "You're just like everyone else. Human. You forget things. We all forget things. It happens. Tell Nicole to get over it."

But Kate wouldn't be comforted. She shouldn't have forgotten the concert. It was important to Nicole. And it was clearly marked on the calendar with a bright red felt-tip pen, so you couldn't miss it.

Except she *had* missed it. Probably because she was so busy feeling sorry for herself she'd forgotten that her first priority, *always*, had to be her children. All of her children. Not just Erin.

So she sent Erin off for the weekend with Linda. And Kate went to the concert and heard Nicole sing. Tom and Tessa went, too. And afterward, Kate took the three of them to dinner at Slater's. She even ordered a bottle of sparkling wine and allowed Nicole to have a half glass. During dessert, she reached into her purse and removed a small, beautifully wrapped box and gave it to Nicole.

"I'm proud of you," she said. "I wanted you to have something special to remember tonight."

Nicole's eyes widened as she accepted the box. When she unwrapped it and saw the delicate gold chain and diamond heart pendant, she gasped. "Mom! It's gorgeous. Thank you! Can I put it on?"

Kate smiled. "Of course."

Later, as they drove home, Kate thought that the

money, used wisely, could smooth away a lot of problems. The trick was to figure out what was wise and what wasn't.

One thing she knew for sure. When it came to her kids, she'd do whatever it took, spend whatever it took, to make them happy.

CHAPTER 13

"You're looking particularly nice today, Kate."

Kate smiled at Keith Ambrose. "Thank you." They'd fallen into the habit of having lunch together anytime she came to Austin. She'd call him the day before, say she was coming, and if he was free, they'd meet at a restaurant of her choice.

Today they were lunching at Carrabba's, and Kate had just enjoyed a wonderful mushroom risotto and some lovely wine that Keith had chosen.

"You seem more relaxed, too," he said. "Have things quieted down a bit?"

"Not exactly. We're no longer bothered by people camping out on our doorstep, but there have been daily traumas at home. Honestly, this win has definitely been a mixed blessing. It's affected my kids a lot more than I expected it to. I mean, I was prepared for people wanting a piece of me. What I wasn't prepared for was the kids' friends wanting a piece of *them*." She sighed. "I don't know. Maybe some of the turmoil is simply due to teenage angst." She smiled ruefully. "I *do* have four teenagers. Sometimes I forget that."

"I know exactly what you mean." His smile was understanding. "I remember when Celia and Doug were teenagers."

In the past weeks, Kate had learned that, like her, Keith was divorced. He had two grown children and had told her the last time they'd lunched together that his daughter, Celia, was engaged and planning to be married in June.

"If I seem more relaxed," Kate said, "it's because I've made a decision. And I made it without consulting my team."

"Oh?"

"I've decided when school's out, the kids and I need to get away."

"That's not a decision where you need input from us, surely."

Kate started to answer just as their waiter approached with the dessert menu. Neither she nor Keith wanted dessert, but they did want coffee. Once the waiter left them alone again, Kate said, "Well, you haven't heard what I'm thinking of doing."

"Taking the kids around the world?"

She grinned. "Nothing quite so exotic. No, I'm thinking of buying an RV and just taking off for the summer. And…from the research I've done…the kind of RV I'm looking at is going to cost a fairly large amount."

Keith studied her for a moment. When he spoke, his voice was wistful. "You know, I've dreamed about doing the very same thing when I retire."

"Have you?"

"Yes. There's something about the open road that's really appealing."

"I know. And when you're somebody like me, who's hardly ever been anywhere, it's *really* appealing." She refolded her napkin. "We just need to get away from everything. The kids and I need to connect as a family again without all the outside pressure caused by the money."

"I think you've made a good decision, Kate. And if you want help choosing an RV, I'd love to tag along."

"Would you? That would be great. It's a big chunk to spend and I'd love another opinion."

The following Friday, Keith took the day off, and the two of them went RV shopping. Kate already had a pretty good idea of what she wanted; she'd done a lot of research online. They went to several dealers—one near Cranbrook, the other two in Austin.

By the end of the day, Kate had chosen a thirty-seven-foot beauty with four slides. Technically, it only slept four, but the bedroom had enough floor space when the slides were pulled out to put a narrow air mattress on the floor, which Nicole could have. Erin would share Kate's bed, and Tessa would have the sofa while Tom slept on another air mattress on the floor in the living area. They could manage.

She swallowed at the price tag, which was close to a quarter million, then figured what the heck. She had the money. And her family needed this getaway. It was worth it. Besides, she'd have the RV to use again and again.

"I'm envious," Keith said when she'd signed the papers and written her check. "Where do you figure you'll go?"

"I don't know. West, probably."

Kate could hardly wait to tell the kids. That night, she waited until they were all seated at the dinner table. Then she tapped her water glass with her fork and when she had their attention, said, "I have a surprise."

Four pairs of curious eyes met hers. Erin grinned. She was always ready for a surprise.

Kate reached for the brochure she'd put under her place mat. "This is what I bought today. It'll be ready for pickup late next week."

"Omigod!" Tessa said.

"*Really*, Mom?" Nicole said.

Tom whistled.

Erin squealed. "Are we gonna go on a trip in it?"

"Yes, we are," Kate said. The kids' excitement had fueled her own, which had already been pretty much off the charts. "Just as soon as school is out. We're going out west for the entire summer."

"The entire *summer!*" Tom said. "But..."

"What, honey?" Kate asked.

He seemed about to say something, then shook his head. "Nothing. It's not important."

"If it's your job you're worried about, you'd be quitting in August, anyway."

"I know," he said. "Don't worry about it, Mom."

Kate smiled. "I think we deserve a summer of fun. Plus I really think it's important that we get away from here…from everything. Don't you?" She looked around the table.

"But what about Ginger and Taffy?" Erin asked, her eyes already worried about the animals.

"Ginger can come with us. And Linda has offered to keep Taffy while we're gone."

Erin bit her lip.

"Honey, we can't take Taffy with us," Kate said gently. "You know how she hates the motion of the car. And Linda loves her. She'll take good care of her."

"I know, but—"

"She'll be *fine*," Nicole said, rolling her eyes.

"Oh, shut up, Nicole," Erin said.

"Girls, please don't fight."

"She's such a baby," Nicole mumbled, ducking when Erin threw her napkin at her.

"Will you two stop it?" Tom said.

"I think this is a *wonderful* idea, Mom," Tessa said. "We'll have so much *fun*. Where out west are we going? California?"

"I don't care. I bought an atlas today. You can look

at it and make a list of places you might like to see, then Tom can help me figure out a driving plan. After that, we can research RV parks where we might like to stay."

For the next few nights, the upcoming trip was all the kids talked about. There were spirited arguments— they called them discussions—about the relative merits of a southern trip that would include New Mexico, Arizona and California versus a northern trip through Colorado and on to Wyoming and Montana.

"I'm so jealous," Linda said. "I wish I was going with you."

"I do, too," Kate said. "But who would watch Taffy for us if you did?" Secretly she was glad Linda wasn't coming. This was family time, and Kate thought it was important that she and the kids were alone. "Besides, you and I will do this another time, just the two of us."

"Promise?" Linda said.

"I promise."

After consulting with Adam Marino, Kate had also decided to buy herself a Jeep Wrangler to tow, because there would be places they'd want to see along the way where they wouldn't want to take the RV. Adam, too, expressed envy over her plans. "I'd give anything to take the summer off and explore like you're going to do."

Kate had put off telling her mother and sisters, but eventually she simply had to. She decided she would take the sting out of the news by giving them each something fun to look forward to, too.

She called them individually to tell them—her mother first.

"I don't need a fancy trip," her mother said stiffly. "I'd rather you'd give the money to the church building fund."

"Mom," Kate said with a sigh, "you know how I feel about that."

"Oh, yes, I know. You've certainly told me enough times."

"If you want to cash in this trip and give the money to the fund, feel free to do so," Kate finally said tiredly. She simply couldn't win where her mother was concerned, so she might as well quit trying.

Kate's sisters were more enthusiastic, but even there, Kate sensed an underlying disappointment and knew they expected a lot more than a week-long cruise. She almost told them she had Keith investigating annuities for them, but stopped herself just in time. What if she changed her mind? Best to wait and think this decision through carefully. Besides, she had a feeling they wouldn't like the idea of an annuity—they'd want a big lump sum of money outright—and right now, Kate simply wasn't up for another argument.

Mark also gave her grief, but his complaint was about the trip she and the kids were taking. "It's not fair to take the kids away for the entire summer," he said. "You know I wanted to take Erin to Disney World."

"I'm sorry, Mark. I had forgotten all about that.

Maybe Erin could fly to meet you and then come back to wherever we are after your trip is over," Kate offered. "When did you want to go?"

"I don't know yet. We're still thinking about it."

"Well, we'll only be a phone call away. When you decide what you're doing, just let me know, and I'll arrange for Erin to be there, too."

After that, there wasn't anything else he could say. Kate knew he would have liked to find something else to object to, but only because he was still angry with her. Too bad, she thought. She refused to allow any of them—her mother, her sisters and, most particularly, Mark—to dampen her enthusiasm or ruin any part of the upcoming trip.

They were going.

And she couldn't wait.

Tom couldn't wait until they left for their trip. Of course, that still wouldn't stop Lucy from calling him or e-mailing him. Geez, he wished he'd never started dating her. If he'd had any idea she was like this, he never would have.

Part of this is your fault. If you hadn't been so quick to jump into bed with her…

But how was he to know she was thinking of love when he was just thinking of sex? He had never even *hinted* that he loved her.

Well, he'd learned a lesson. He wasn't gonna date

any girl more than twice from now on. Who needed that kind of problem? And if Lucy didn't quit calling him, he might just have to get a new cell phone with a number she didn't know.

Two days before they were scheduled to leave on their trip, Kate and Tom took delivery on the new motor coach. Tessa drove them to the dealership and Kate let Tom drive the vehicle back to Cranbrook. They'd all three taken the classes on how to operate it, but she and Tessa had agreed beforehand that Tom could have the honors. He'd pretended he wasn't nervous, but Kate knew he was.

He drove carefully, though, and by the time they got back to the house, he was driving like an old pro. Kate and Tessa would get their practice the next day.

It was the last day of school for Erin and Nicole, and when they arrived home, they squealed with excitement as they explored the compact interior. Later, after an easy dinner of hamburgers and salad, they went over their checklist and began carrying provisions out to the coach.

"You won't need much," Kate warned, "so keep it light. We've got the washer and dryer, remember. If you need something you don't have, we can always buy it."

That night, Linda came by to pick up Taffy and all of her paraphernalia. Erin got weepy when she had to say goodbye to the cat. Nicole started to make a disparaging remark, but Kate gave her a look that said, *Don't you dare*, and she clamped her mouth shut.

Linda gave them all hugs. "Have a wonderful time."

"We intend to," Kate said.

"E-mail me as often as you can."

Kate had purchased a laptop computer with a wireless connection, so they'd be in easy touch. "I will. But hey, we'll probably be talking every day. We do have cell phones, you know."

"I know." Linda's expression was wistful.

Kate felt a pang of regret. In many ways, she *did* wish Linda was going with them even as she knew it was best for their family to be alone this summer.

After Linda left, Kate finished cleaning out the refrigerator while Tom and Tessa practiced hitching and unhitching the Jeep and continued to study the owner's manual.

Finally they were ready, and everyone went to bed. Kate knew she'd be too excited to sleep much, but she was more tired than she'd realized. The last she remembered was the digital clock at her bedside reading a few minutes past midnight.

The next morning, they were up at six. They didn't bother with breakfast. They would eat on the road. Kate fixed herself a cup of instant coffee while Tom backed the RV out to the street and parked it in front of the house. While Kate took one last look around, Tom and Tessa got the Jeep hooked up to the hitch.

"Do you want to drive first, Mom?" Tom asked.

Kate smiled. She knew he was dying to take the

driver's seat. "No, that's okay. You go first. I'll drive when you need a break."

Their route today would take them south to Interstate 10, then west toward El Paso. They planned to stop for the night in Fort Stockton, Texas. Today's route was approximately three hundred miles, and Kate figured they'd easily be there by early afternoon. She didn't want to be on the road more than six or seven hours in any one day. In fact, the book she'd bought about RV trips recommended not driving more than two hundred miles in any given day, the point being that you were supposed to enjoy the journey itself and not race to any particular destination.

Ginger, after sniffing every nook and cranny of the coach, settled down in the front between Tom's and Kate's seats. Nicole went back to sleep after instructing them to wake her when they stopped for breakfast. Tessa sat at the table with that day's Sudoku puzzle from the paper. And Erin curled up with a book.

As Tom eased the coach onto the highway and they headed away from Cranbrook, Kate smiled. She could already feel the tension and worry of the past months slipping away.

This was the best idea she'd had in a long time. And maybe, by the time the summer was over, she'd have a better handle on how to deal with her lottery win and all the problems that had come along with it.

CHAPTER 14

After covering three hundred miles the first day, they took it easier the next two days, although with three of them able to operate the coach, no one had to drive more than a couple of hours at a stretch. It didn't matter. They weren't in any particular hurry. They had two and a half months and no set schedule, so they might as well take their time.

Kate was enthralled once they entered New Mexico. She quickly understood why it was called the Land of Enchantment. The colors alone were a feast for the eyes: indigo, violet, umber, loden, magenta, tangerine, goldenrod, all under a sky so blue it almost hurt to look at it. The landscape fascinated her. It was so different from Cranbrook and the Austin and San Antonio areas.

Here were mesas and mountains, cactus and agaves. She had purchased a book that described the terrain and identified the trees, plants, flowers and animal life. She was constantly referring to it when Tom or Tessa was driving.

"Look!" she would exclaim. "That's a mariposa," or, "That's a Corkbark fir," or, "That's a cottonwood tree."

The kids humored her for a while, looking politely and making appropriately appreciative sounds, but they quickly lost interest and would go back to their card game or book or iPod. Kate didn't mind. She was having fun.

They were no longer on the interstate. After El Paso, they'd moved to secondary roads. They couldn't drive as fast, but that didn't matter. The scenery was more interesting, and it was certainly less stressful because they'd pretty much left behind all the big trucks and speed demons.

In researching campsites, Kate had found one near Santa Fe that looked wonderful. Called Juniper Park Campsite, it was nestled on the shore of a small lake in a wooded area. The Web site listed all the amenities, which included horseback riding and lessons at a nearby stable, tennis, badminton, swimming at both the on-site pool and in the lake, canoeing, fishing, mountain biking and hiking.

"You're in luck," the manager had said when she called. "Just this morning one of our customers had a family emergency and had to give up his site. If you want it, it's yours."

He had agreed to hold it for them if she would guarantee him a two-week stay. After conferring with the kids, she'd agreed.

When they pulled into the entrance to Juniper Park, Kate knew they'd really been lucky to find this place. The campsite was beautiful—clean and well kept and even nicer than it had looked on its Web site. She paid the manager for the agreed-upon two weeks, with the proviso that they might want to stay longer.

"It's yours as long as you want it," he said. A big redhead in his late forties or early fifties, he had a friendly smile and reassuring manner that immediately made Kate feel at ease. Since they were still new to RVing, he sent his teenage son, whose name was Nathan, to show them where everything was located and to help them with their utility hookups.

Their site was fairly close to the office and lake, which Kate liked. They were the third coach in a row of ten, with an equal number of sites across a paved roadway.

As they were letting out their slides and removing their lawn chairs from the outside storage bin, their neighbors to the right came out and introduced themselves. Fred and Cindy Alston were a sixtysomething retired couple who were full-time RVers, they told Kate. Fred was tall and thin, with sparse dark hair, rimless glasses and lively dark eyes, while his wife was short and compact, with curly white hair and light-blue eyes. Both were tanned and fit-looking.

"What a nice bunch of kids you've got," Fred said, watching as Tom and Tessa arranged the furniture on the side of the coach and Erin took Ginger for a walk.

Nicole, of course, was conveniently in the bathroom. She always seemed to disappear when there was work to be done. Kate was going to have to do something about that girl soon. She'd put it off too long already.

"Ours are all grown and gone now," Cindy said. "But a couple of our grandchildren are going to join us for two weeks later this month."

"Oh, that'll be nice," Kate said.

Cindy beamed, eyes alight. "We can't wait. We don't get to see much of them because they live in Chicago and we live in Dallas."

"Really? We're from the Austin area."

"I figured you were fellow Texans," Fred said. "From your license plates."

Before Kate knew it, they were chatting away like old friends. At one point, Cindy went into their coach and came back out with a plate of sugar cookies and a big pitcher of lemonade. She set it down on the picnic table between their coaches. The cookies and lemonade drew Kate's kids like a magnet. Even Nicole deigned to come out and join them.

"You'd think they'd never eaten before," Kate said, watching as the cookies quickly disappeared.

Cindy smiled. "Don't you wish you could still eat like that?" Then she made a face. "Sorry. Maybe *you* still can. I just know I can't."

"Believe me, I can't, either," Kate said.

"So where do you think the stables are, Mom?" Tessa asked, looking around. "I'd love to go check them out."

Fred pointed toward the forested area on the other side of the RV park. "Just past those trees you'll see a path that goes straight to them," he said. "It's about a ten-minute walk."

"Oh, Mom, can we go see?" Erin asked. She was so excited at the prospect, she was practically jumping up and down.

"Um…" Kate hesitated.

"It's perfectly safe," Fred said, guessing what she was thinking. "Our grandkids are only ten and twelve, and we let them walk over by themselves all the time."

"Well," Kate said, "I guess it's okay. But take your cell phone, Tessa, and call me if there's any problem, okay?"

Tessa refrained from rolling her eyes, although Kate knew she wanted to. "I will."

"And don't go too near the horses," Kate warned, knowing how Erin was about any animal, large or small.

"Mom…" Erin said with a long-suffering sigh.

Cindy chuckled. "Mothers are supposed to worry. It's part of the rules of motherhood."

Tessa grinned and nudged Erin. "Erin's just as bad, only she worries about the sky falling."

"I do *not!*"

"If we're going, let's go," Tom said.

Once the kids had gone, Cindy and Fred continued telling Kate about the camp and the many attractions within an hour or two driving time. "Of course, you must get into Santa Fe as often as you can," Cindy said. "It's a wonderful town. Especially if you like art."

"Tessa would really enjoy that," Kate said.

"And Los Alamos is worth seeing, too," Fred put in.

Before he had a chance to elaborate, the people in the space across from them rode up in a Jeep similar to Kate's. Cindy waved them over, saying, "Come meet our new neighbor."

Shirley and Mitch DeSilva were also full-time RVers, and they were just as friendly as the Alstons. It was immediately obvious to Kate that the two couples were fast friends and had stayed here and at other RV parks together in the past. After talking a while, Shirley suggested that Kate and her children join them for a community cookout that night.

"We'll supply hot dogs and buns," Shirley said. She was a plump blonde with a beautiful smile. "And I made a macaroni salad this morning, so I'll bring that, too."

"I can put together a green salad," Cindy said. "And I've got half a watermelon I can contribute."

"I was just going to feed the kids sandwiches and chips tonight, so I didn't take anything out of the freezer, but I can open a couple of cans of corn and bring chips and dip," Kate said.

"Perfect," Cindy said. Turning to Shirley, she added, "Why don't we ask Gabe to join us?"

"Good idea," Shirley said. "I'll walk down there now. I see his truck, so I'm pretty sure he's there."

"Gabe is our resident hunk," Cindy said to Kate.

Shirley came back a few minutes later. "He says thanks, he'll be here. And he says he'll bring baked beans and a chocolate cake he baked this morning."

A man who baked. Now that sounded interesting.

"Shirley and I have been trying to figure Gabe out ever since he got here," Cindy said. "I mean, he's friendly, but he hasn't volunteered a lot of information about himself, and we're curious. Thing is, he's pretty young, I'm guessing early fifties, and he's traveling alone, and from what we can tell, he doesn't work." Cindy lowered her voice so the men, who had drifted off a ways and were deep in conversation about something, couldn't hear her. "He's also really sexy." Her smile turned devilish. "Shirley and I agreed he could put his shoes under our beds anytime."

Kate joined in their laughter.

"Are *you* married, Kate?" Shirley asked.

"Uh-oh, matchmaker at work," Cindy warned.

"I'm divorced," Kate said.

"Gun-shy?" Shirley said.

"No, not really. I haven't dated much the past seven years, but recently I've gotten my feet wet again." She made a face. "It's kind of scary to start dating again."

"This is my second marriage," Shirley said, "and I remember how nervous I was the first time I went out on a date after *my* divorce."

"I can't even imagine," Cindy said.

Soon after, the kids returned, full of excitement over the "awesome stables, Mom," and "the really cool horses." This seemed to be the impetus to break up the group and, after agreeing they'd all meet outside at six, everyone went into their respective coaches.

Tom told his mom he was going for a walk. "I kind of want to see what all's here." He would have asked Tessa if she wanted to go with him, but she had fallen asleep on Kate's bed, so he struck off on his own.

He hadn't gone ten yards when his cell phone rang. Checking the number, he saw it was Lucy, and he decided to let the call go to voice mail. He was *sick* of her calling him. Why couldn't she get the *message?* Was she *stupid?* Any guilt over hurting her had long since faded under the onslaught of her constant harassment.

He walked toward the lake where he watched some kids diving off the pier. Geez, this was beautiful country. He loved it here already. Maybe he should have applied to a college in New Mexico. Of course, if he got accepted at Columbia—which he still hadn't heard from—that would still be his first choice.

He loved the weather here, though. It was warm, but there was no humidity—so different from home. He sat on a bench and smiled at the kids' antics.

He sighed, thinking about Lucy's call. Surely she

wouldn't keep this up much longer. She was bound to get tired of calling him and stop. Wishing he knew what to do to get rid of her now, he took his cell phone out of the right front pocket of his cargo shorts. Might as well get it over with. Listen to her message, then delete it.

Tom!

Oh, shit. She was crying. Again.

Tom, you'd better call me back, and right away or I'm going to call your aunt and get your mother's cell phone number and then I'll call her and tell her I'm pregnant.

Tom's hand shook, his heart thumped like someone banging on a bass drum and his mind spun.

Pregnant!

How could she be *pregnant?*

And if your aunt won't give me the number, I'll tell her I'm pregnant and you're the father. And don't think I won't!

Now she was crying so hard she was hiccuping.

And you'd better not try to say you're not the father, Tom, because you know you are.

Shock reverberated through him. Lucy had said she was on the Pill! What had happened?

He swallowed, hard. Snapped the phone closed. Got up and walked aimlessly as his mind continued to go in circles. What was he going to do? He had no doubt Lucy had told him the truth. She was pregnant.

And I'm the father.

He thought about college. The degree he wanted to get. The work he wanted to do. He thought about his family. His mom, especially. She would be so disappointed in him. He thought about his grandparents. His dad. They'd *all* be disappointed in him.

Tears threatened, but he forced them back.

What was he going to do?

He didn't want to call Lucy back. Not now. Not anytime soon. He wanted to calm down, think about this, figure out his options and talk to Tessa. But he knew he didn't dare wait, because Lucy had shown him how unstable she was, and he knew she would follow through on her threat. If he didn't call her back soon, she *would* get his mother's cell number.

Feeling more helpless than he'd ever felt in his life, he opened the phone again and pressed in her number.

A few minutes before six, the kids carried out Kate's dinner contribution while she finished dressing. Knowing it would cool off later, she put on cropped pants instead of shorts and tied a fleece hoodie around her waist. Then she uncorked a bottle of her favorite shiraz and went out to join the group.

Fred and Cindy were already outside, with Cindy busy arranging food on the picnic table while Fred talked to a man Kate assumed must be the unknown Gabe. Studying him covertly, she agreed with Shirley and Cindy. He *was* sexy. Also quite attractive, in a rugged, outdoorsy way. He was tall, even taller than Fred, with a strong, athletic build and broad shoulders.

"Great minds," Cindy said, smiling at the wine Kate held. "I brought some out, too."

At the sound of her voice, the men turned.

"Here she is," Fred said. "Kate, come meet Gabe."

Kate walked over to join them.

"Kate Bishop, Gabe Fletcher," Fred said.

Kate looked up into a pair of the bluest eyes she'd ever seen. "Hi. It's nice to meet you." She stuck out her hand.

"It's nice to meet you, too."

They shook hands and smiled at each other. It was funny, Kate decided later, how she'd known instantly that she and Gabe would be friends. There was just something about him that said he was the kind of person she would enjoy knowing.

Just then Shirley and Mitch walked over, and in the bustle of adding their food to the table and getting Fred's grill ready to cook the hot dogs, Kate and Gabe drifted apart. But she continued to study him surreptitiously, especially when he went out of his way to talk to Tom.

She frowned.

Something was wrong with Tom. When he'd come back from his walk, it was obvious to Kate that something had happened. She wondered if it had to do with Lucy, the girl he'd dated earlier this year. Tessa had told Kate they'd broken up, but Kate knew Lucy had called him several times over the past weeks. Once she'd overheard part of their conversation—at least from

Tom's end—and it was clear he was unhappy. Did he still care for her? Was that the problem? She wished he would confide in her the way he used to when he was little. She sighed. What she really wanted was for her kids to either hurry and grow up and get past all this angst, or else revert back to being younger and just stay there. She remembered reading something once about little kids, little problems, big kids, big problems.

"Penny for your thoughts," Cindy said.

Kate made a determined effort to put Tom and his problem out of her mind for the rest of the evening. She filled a plate, found a place to sit and mostly listened to the lively conversation around her.

She noticed that Gabe mostly listened, too, although he and Erin talked for a long time about her desire to be a vet one day. Kate only heard snatches of their conversation because she was at the other end of the table, but during a brief lull she heard Gabe say, "My son used to talk about veterinary school."

So he *had* been married.

"What happened?" Erin asked. "Did he change his mind?"

Gabe hesitated, then said softly, "No. He died his senior year in high school."

Not everyone had heard what he'd said, but Kate had. *Oh, God.* Losing a child had to be the worst possible thing that could ever happen to a parent. Her heart hurt for him.

Erin looked stricken, and Kate wished she was closer to her, because she knew Erin didn't know what to say. Tessa, who was sitting next to Kate, bit her lip.

By now, everyone seemed to feel the strange tension in the air, and the other conversations died away.

"I'm so sorry, Gabe," Shirley said.

He nodded. "It's been fifteen years. I've learned to deal with it." Giving himself an almost visible shake, he smiled at Erin. "Tony would have made a great vet, and so will you."

Erin smiled uncertainly, but Gabe continued to talk to her about veterinary medicine, and gradually her discomfort seemed to fade.

Gabe's revelation fueled Kate's curiosity about him. Now she wondered what had happened to his marriage. Had his wife died, too? Or were they divorced? Kate knew the death of a child put tremendous strain on a marriage. Even good ones felt it, and if there was any kind of fissure in the relationship, it had a tough time surviving the trauma.

The talk turned to the life of a full-timer, which both the Alstons and the DeSilvas were. From there, the conversation segued to Kate.

"How long are you planning to stay at Juniper, Kate?" The questioner was Shirley.

Kate shrugged. "We aren't sure. I paid for two weeks, but if we like it here, we may stay longer." Seeing the curious looks, she added, "We're planning to be away until school starts, but we've left our schedule pretty flexible."

"Did you take a leave of absence from your job?" Shirley said. "Or are you a stay-at-home mom?"

Kate was prepared for this question, knowing it would come sooner or later. "Until a few months ago, I worked as the office manager in a doctor's office." She knew they were probably all wondering how she could afford the kind of motor coach they were driving. Maybe they'd think she had a wealthy ex-husband or something. "Now I'm temporarily unemployed."

Tessa looked at her in surprise. "Are you thinking of going back to work, Mom?"

"I'm sure I will, honey. Once all of you are back in school, I'd be bored silly at home all the time."

Tessa knew not to say anything about the lottery. All the kids did. Kate hoped they wouldn't forget, because the last thing she wanted was for anyone they met this summer to know. She was enjoying the peace and anonymity far too much.

"I don't miss working at all," Shirley said.

"What did you used to do?" Kate asked.

"I taught the fourth grade for thirty-eight years."

"My mother was a teacher, too," Kate said. "So I know just how difficult a job it is."

"I don't miss working, either," Mitch said. "In fact, I couldn't wait to retire."

Gabe had been quiet through this exchange. Kate

glanced his way and wondered what he was thinking. "What about you, Gabe?" she said. "Are you retired, too?"

"Temporarily."

"He told us he's still trying to figure out what he wants to be when he grows up," Cindy said, grinning.

Gabe just smiled.

"What did you do before you temporarily retired?" Kate asked.

"I was in the computer software business."

Kate would have loved to ask more questions, but she felt she'd been nosy enough. When they got to know each other better, maybe he'd volunteer more.

By now the kids had gotten restive. Even the twins could only sit still so long. Nicole asked if they could go inside the coach and watch one of the movies they'd brought along, and Kate said that would be fine, but first they'd have to help clean up. She eyed Tom. He still seemed preoccupied.

After the kids went inside, Kate continued to sit outdoors with the others. The men had gotten into a spirited discussion of the current baseball season. Fred admitted he still followed the Cleveland Indians, Gabe was a Mariners fan, and Mitch just enjoyed the game itself without rooting for any particular team. Kate enjoyed listening to them and their easy banter and good-natured disagreements as to the merits of different players and coaches. She had forgotten how nice it was to be in the company of men who liked each other's company and didn't have any axes to grind.

Eventually, though, the long day caught up with Kate. After she found herself yawning repeatedly, she said, "I think I'm going to have to say good night. I'm beat."

Just as she stood, the screen door to her coach opened, and Erin came out, followed by Nicole. "Mom, we were talking, and we want to go horseback riding tomorrow morning, okay?" Erin said.

"We'll discuss it when I come inside, honey."

"But, Mom—"

"When I come inside, Erin," Kate said more firmly. She wasn't sure about horseback riding. The kids had never been on a horse. Neither had she. Horseback riding could be dangerous if you didn't know what you were doing.

"You're gonna say no, aren't you?" Nicole said.

Kate sighed.

The screen door opened again and Tessa said, "It's perfectly safe, Mom. They give beginner lessons over there and everything."

"What's worrying you, Kate?" Cindy asked.

For just a moment, Kate was irritated. These were *her* kids. If she was worried about something, it was her business. After all, she'd only met Cindy today. She wasn't obligated to explain anything to her.

But just as quickly as the irritation formed, it dissipated, because these people had been very nice to her, and she already knew they were sensible and normal.

"None of us has ever been on a horse," she said.

"The horses Sam and his wife use for inexperienced riders are gentle," Fred said. "Our grandkids had no previous riding experience, either, and they did just fine last year."

"I rode last year," Shirley said, "and trust me, there's no one greener or more inept than me."

"That's for sure," Mitch said, then ducked as she tried to swat him.

"If it would make you feel better, Kate," Gabe said, "I'll go with them. I've been riding all my life."

Still Kate hesitated.

"You can come, too, Mom," Tessa said.

"You promised us adventure," Nicole reminded her.

"Yeah, Mom," Erin said.

Kate noticed Tom had not joined the girls. "Does your brother want to go, too?"

"Tom," Tessa called. "Are you going with us in the morning?" Turning back to Kate, she said, "He said yes."

Kate knew when she was beaten. She sighed again. "Oh, all right." Turning to Gabe, she said, "Are you sure you don't mind?"

"I'm sure. In fact, I'm looking forward to it."

When he smiled at her, Kate felt a little zing in her stomach. She knew Gabe liked her…that he was as intrigued by her as she was by him. For the first time in months, she didn't have to question what had prompted that interest, either, for Gabe didn't know about the lottery win. He liked her for herself.

But the tingling anticipation of Gabe's company during the excursion the next morning disappeared as Kate, with the girls following, walked into the coach and saw Tom sitting staring into space. The expression on his face—which he quickly tried to banish with a smile—caused a pulse of alarm.

He'd looked so *forlorn*. As if his best friend had died. What could have made him look that way?

Unfortunately, one of the drawbacks of their close quarters was a lack of privacy, so she couldn't talk to him tonight. But tomorrow, first chance she got, she was determined to find out what was wrong.

She simply had to.

She couldn't stand seeing him like this.

CHAPTER 15

"What are you going to do?" Tessa asked.

"I don't know."

She and Tom were talking in low tones because they didn't want to wake the others, even though the door to the bedroom was shut. Tessa felt terrible for Tom, yet somehow she wasn't surprised. She'd had a bad feeling about Lucy for a while now. "Do you think there's any chance she's not telling you the truth?" she said after a moment.

"Why would she do that?"

"Tom. Think about it. Girls *have* been known to lie about a pregnancy to get a man to marry them."

"But that doesn't make sense. If she's lying, she knows I'll find out about it eventually. I mean, there won't be any baby."

"By then it would be too late."

"Well, it doesn't matter whether she's lying. Because no matter what Lucy says, I'm not gonna marry her."

He spoke with more determination in his voice than Tessa had heard there in a long time when the subject was Lucy. "Look, Tom, I know you don't want to tell Mom, but you have to. She'll find out, anyway."

"Yeah," he said disconsolately.

"The sooner you tell her, the better it'll be."

He sighed heavily.

"Because she'll know what to do."

"Is that gonna be before or after she kills me?"

"She's not gonna kill you. She'll be pretty upset, but she'll get over it."

Ginger, who always slept between the two front seats, stirred just then and whimpered in her sleep.

Tessa smiled. Ginger was having a dream. "You know, I just thought of something. Maybe all Lucy really wants is money."

"Money?"

"Yeah, like everyone else since Mom won the lottery. Maybe she sees this as her chance to get a big chunk." Warming to her subject, she said, "Think about it, Tom. She knows Mom thinks you're wonderful. She might just think Mom would be happy to pay her off."

"Think so?"

Tessa heard the hopeful note. "It's very possible."

"Do…you think Mom *would* pay her off?"

"Yes. Don't you?"

"I don't know. She might be so disappointed in me she won't want to make it easier for me. You know how she's always saying we need to take responsibility for our decisions and not try to blame anyone else when something happens." The hopeful note was gone.

"But this is too serious, Tom. It'll affect the rest of your life. Mom will help. You'll see."

He was silent for a long time. When he spoke, he sounded resigned. "What I *should* do is forget about going away to school, see if I can have my job with the nursery back—I'll bet Jimmy hasn't found anybody to replace me yet—and take classes at night at the community college. That way I could give Lucy child support money."

"Mom won't want you to do that, Tom. Not when we have so much money. It would be crazy."

"I didn't say I wanted to do it. But it would be the right thing, wouldn't it?"

Tessa had always known Tom was one of the good guys. She reached over the side of the sofa and squeezed his shoulder. "I love you," she whispered.

"Yeah," he said with a catch in his voice. "Love you, too."

When Kate awakened, she slipped out of bed, stepped around Erin, and quietly let herself out of the bedroom. One of the drawbacks to having so many people in the RV was the fact she couldn't get into the kitchen area to make coffee without disturbing the twins. But knowing them, even if she did wake them, they'd go right back to sleep. She smiled. What was it about reaching the teen years that changed a kid from waking at dawn to sleeping like the dead until you forced them out of bed?

Fifteen minutes later, carrying a mugful of hot coffee in one hand and Ginger's leash in the other, she walked outside. The early morning air was cool and felt good. She waited until Ginger had relieved herself in the grass, then opened the door of the coach again and urged the dog back inside, even though she didn't want to go. Kate ignored her mournful eyes, saying softly, "It's too early for you to be out. People are still sleeping."

Walking slowly as she sipped her coffee, Kate headed down the roadway, studying the different coaches as she passed them. Most were as big or bigger than hers. And, as she'd thought, there wasn't much sign of life in them.

"'Morning."

The greeting was soft, but startled her nevertheless, and she nearly spilled her coffee. Whipping around, she saw Gabe leaning against his coach. He, too, held a mug of what she assumed must be coffee. "Good morning. I didn't see you there."

"I know. I tried not to scare you." He smiled. "You're up early."

"You, too."

He nodded, taking another drink of his coffee. "I like mornings."

"They're my favorite time of day."

"So…are you ready for the horseback riding later?"

She chuckled. "I'm still not sure I want to entrust my body to the vagaries of an animal, but since I can't get out of it without my kids having a fit, I guess I am."

He laughed. "I like an honest woman."

Their eyes met and held, and Kate found herself forgetting to breathe. What was it about this man that she found so compelling? He was sexy, yes, but she'd been around sexy men before who hadn't caused this kind of visceral reaction.

Rattled, she looked away and told her body to behave. Geez. Maybe she'd been without a man in her life for so long her hormones were skewed. Maybe, right now, she'd be drawn to just about any reasonably attractive specimen.

Yet even as she thought it, she knew that wasn't true. She certainly didn't feel this way when she was with Keith Ambrose, and he was *more* than reasonably attractive. No, this reaction had to do with Gabe.

What about Adam? You go all goofy when you're around him, too.

And what did *that* say about her?

"So what time would you like to get going?" Gabe asked.

Forcing her mind away from its current path, she said, "I probably won't be able to budge my kids before nine. Is ten too late?"

He shook his head. "Ten is perfect." He looked

down at her flip-flops. "I don't suppose you've got a pair of boots."

"No. Is that a prerequisite?"

"Don't sound so hopeful."

Kate grinned.

"It's certainly safer," he said. "But I'm sure half the folks who ride over at Sam's don't have boots to wear."

"Why are boots safer?"

"They protect your feet. Even the heel has a function. It keeps your foot from sliding all the way through the stirrup."

"Oh. Then maybe we *shouldn't* ride without them."

"You'll be fine. Just wear socks and your sturdiest shoes."

"That would be sneakers, I'm afraid."

"And don't wear shorts. Everyone should wear jeans or another pair of long pants. Otherwise, the insides of your legs will be rubbed raw, which isn't pleasant."

"I guess not." Kate drank the last bit of her coffee. "Well, since I can't get out of this, I guess I'll see you later."

Gabe smiled. "Looking forward to it."

Tom wondered if he should tell his mom about Lucy before they went riding or wait until afterward when it might be easier to get her off alone. Right now she was busy making breakfast for everyone and by the time they finished eating, Gabe would probably be here.

He guessed he'd have to wait. He hated waiting, though. The news was like a lead weight in his stomach. In fact, he wasn't sure he could even eat breakfast.

Yesterday, after calling Lucy back, he'd turned his cell phone off. It was still off. He just couldn't handle talking to her again.

His head hurt from thinking about everything.

Why had he been so stupid?

He'd known Lucy wasn't right for him even before he and Tessa had talked that first time, yet he'd kept putting off making the break. He was a coward. And now he was going to pay for it, big-time.

At one point in their conversation yesterday, Lucy had cried, "I thought you *liked* children, Tom!"

He *did* like kids. And he wanted kids of his own. Someday. That was the key word. Someday.

But when he'd tried to tell Lucy that, she'd said, "Well, I'm so sorry I don't fit your timetable."

Tom sighed.

Hell. It was no use thinking about it. Somehow he'd get through the morning, but right after they were through riding, he was going to tell his mother. He would also tell her he'd come to a decision.

Erin was so happy, she thought she might burst.

Oh, she loved the horses! Especially hers—a horse named Pepper that Josh said was a piebald. Erin loved that name—piebald. Pepper had big black and white splotches on her. Josh had picked her out especially for Erin, saying she was perfect for her. Well, he'd picked out all the horses, but Erin liked hers best.

Josh was so cool. He was also really cute. In fact, he looked like one of those California surfers, all tanned and blond with really white teeth. She could see both Tessa and Nicole thought he was cute, too, seeing how they were acting around him. Josh and his sister, Jenny, were Sam's kids, and they would be taking them out on the trail for their ride.

"You're all going to wear helmets," Jenny was saying.

"Helmets!" Tessa said. "But *why?*"

Josh smiled at Tessa. "For insurance purposes, we make all our riders wear them. Trust me, it's a lot safer that way."

Erin's mom made a face and muttered, "I knew I didn't want to do this."

Gabe, who was standing next to her, chuckled and winked at Erin. "She's worried about her hair," he said.

Jenny smiled. She had red hair and freckles like her father, and Erin liked her, too.

While Jenny had Tom, Tessa and Erin's mom sign releases, Josh helped each of them mount, then adjusted their stirrups. After that, he showed them how to grab hold of the saddle horn and how to sit. First they had to stand up and let their heels drop, and he emphasized how important it was to keep their heels lower than their toes. Then he showed them how to hold the reins. "Like you're holding a water hose," he said. "That's right," he added, smiling at Tessa. Erin could tell he liked her, too. So could Nicole, because she gave Tessa a dirty look. Erin smothered a smile.

"Now remember," Josh was saying, "these horses know what they're doing and where they're going. They've done this hundreds of times. So just let them go. Keep your hand centered over the saddle horn and don't jerk the reins and you'll be fine."

As they set off down the trail—Josh in the lead and Jenny bringing up the rear—Erin decided that this was what heaven must be like. She loved the trees on both sides of the trail and the way they had to duck low-hanging branches. She loved the wild flowers growing in unexpected places. She loved the sounds of the birds and the way there would be unexpected flashes of color as they flew from one tree to another when they passed. She loved the feel of the sun on her shoulders and the crisp New Mexican air, which was so different from the air in Texas. But most of all, she loved Pepper and how she smelled and how it felt to be riding her. It was exactly the way she'd dreamed it would be. It was so wonderful, she didn't want the ride to ever end.

Someday I'll have my own horse. And I won't have to wear sneakers when I'm riding her. I'll have boots and the right kind of hat and I'll ride as fast as the wind....

That was the only disappointment today—how slow they were going. Erin knew it was because they were all beginners and Sam—Josh and Jenny's father—didn't want anyone getting hurt. She also knew before she could ride the way she wanted to, she'd need to take lessons.

She sighed.

What would she have to do to persuade her mom to buy a horse for her? She knew her mom's reluctance had nothing to do with money. After all, they were rich. Her mom could buy anything for them that she wanted to buy.

"How you doing back there?" Josh called, turning to look at them.

Everyone called out that they were fine.

"They're all doing great," Jenny called from the back.

"She's being generous," Erin's mom said.

Gabe laughed. "You're doing great, too, Kate."

"I have a feeling I'm going to be very sore tomorrow," Erin's mom said.

"Did I forget to tell you that?" Josh said, grinning. "You're all going to be sore."

Erin didn't care. She'd be sore every day for the rest of her life if it meant she could have a horse.

All too soon, the ride was over and they were back at the stables. Erin's mom moaned as Gabe helped her dismount.

"My legs feel like spaghetti," she said.

Erin's legs felt like spaghetti, too, but she pretended

they didn't. And she noticed Nicole and Tessa were both trying to impress Josh by acting as if *their* legs were fine. She looked at Tom. He hadn't said much during the ride, and right now, he was standing kind of away from everyone else. Erin frowned. What was wrong with him? He looked funny. Like he was worried, or something. Erin loved Tom. Unlike Nicole, and even sometimes Tessa, he was always nice to her. She hoped he was okay.

But thoughts of Tom quickly disappeared when she heard Josh saying, "I hope you all had fun today, and I hope you'll come back."

"I'm definitely coming back," Tessa said.

"Me, *too*," Nicole said.

Erin didn't say anything. She planned to be there every day, but first she had to work on her mom. She was going to beg, plead, even cry if she had to, because she wanted to sign up for riding lessons. And not just for two weeks, either. For the rest of the summer.

Maybe it was a good thing both Tessa and Nicole were acting so silly over Josh. That meant they'd want to stay here, too. And if all three of them worked on their mom, maybe she'd agree.

That just left Tom.

If Erin could get Tom on their side, too, her mom would be sure to say yes. Erin resolved that as soon as they got back to the coach, she would talk to him. Then, remembering how preoccupied he'd seemed lately, she frowned. What would she do if he wouldn't listen to her? Or if he really wanted to leave here and go to California the way they'd planned?

But she wouldn't think that way.

She would think positive, the way her grandmother was always telling her to, and everything would work out just fine.

CHAPTER 16

Kate was pleased when, on the walk back to the coach, Tom said he needed to talk to her. Now she wouldn't have to approach him. She hoped he planned to confide whatever it was that was troubling him.

Her heart instantly felt lighter. Funny how just knowing your kids felt they could trust you when they had a problem made everything better. "Can it wait till after lunch? I'm sure everyone's hungry."

"Oh. Sure," he said.

She could see he didn't want to wait. "Or maybe Tessa could make sandwiches and while the girls eat, we can go somewhere and talk."

He immediately brightened. "That would be good."

Smiling at him, she said, "Okay. I'll ask her."

Later, after saying goodbye to Gabe and changing from her jeans and sneakers to shorts and sandals, she and Tom set off. She waited for him to initiate the conversation, but he remained silent as they walked. Worry niggled at Kate again. What could it be that was making him look so serious?

When they reached the lake, he pointed to a bench in the shade. Only when they were seated did he take a deep breath and begin to talk.

Kate listened quietly, her heart sinking further and farther with each word. "Oh, Tom," she said when he fell silent again. Her emotions were so turbulent, she wasn't sure what she felt. Shock, disbelief, love, pity, sorrow, disappointment, anger. They were all there.

"I'm sorry, Mom. I—I know I've let you down."

He looked so unhappy, she wanted to say he hadn't, but she knew he wouldn't believe her. Because he *had* let her down. This was the last thing she'd ever expected from him.

And yet…was she *really* so shocked? Didn't accidental pregnancies happen to kids every day? And not just kids…even supposedly responsible adults could have a lapse in judgment in the passion of the moment. But kids were particularly vulnerable, because their hormones went nuts in their teens.

"I won't pretend I'm not disappointed," Kate finally said. "And I won't pretend it's a small thing, either, because it's not. You've made Lucy pregnant and you'll have to take care of it."

Tom looked at her in alarm. "She'll *never* agree to an abortion, Mom."

"That isn't what I meant. I meant you'll have to step up to the plate and do the right thing."

"But I don't love her! And I don't want to marry her."

"I didn't say you should. By doing the right thing, I meant you have to assume your share of responsibility for the baby. And not just financially."

"How? If I don't want to marry her?"

"By being a part of the baby's life. Giving Lucy money isn't enough. Like it or not, you're going to be the baby's father. And that means being involved." Despite her unhappiness over what this mistake might do to Tom's future, Kate couldn't stop the little spark of excitement that had ignited in her belly.

A grandchild…

Kate had always loved babies. She used to laugh when friends would hint that maybe four kids was overkill, saying she kept forgetting babies grew up so she couldn't seem to stop having them.

Forcing these thoughts away, she said, "What do you want to do, Tom?"

"Right now I think I need to go home. And see Lucy in person."

Kate nodded. "And then what?"

"I want her to understand that if she's really pregnant, I'll take my share of responsibility, but I'm not marrying her."

"*Really* pregnant? You mean there's some doubt?"

After Tom explained what Tessa had speculated, Kate nodded again. "I guess it's possible this is just a ploy."

Tom heaved a sigh. "While I'm in Cranbrook, I'm planning to go see Jimmy, ask if I can have my job back."

Kate stared at him. "But why?"

"Because that's the best way for me to help Lucy."

"Tom! What about school?"

"I can still go to school. I can take classes at night at the community college."

"Tom, that's crazy. Good Lord, honey, we have more money than we can ever spend. Why should you give up college? In fact, why should *Lucy?* Okay, you two made a mistake, but two parents without a decent education? Is that what you want for your child? Or any other children you may have in the future?"

"I thought you'd *want* me to do this on my own. I mean, you always tell us we have to accept the consequences when we do something wrong."

Kate put her arm around him. Her anger was gone. This was Tom. He was a good kid. He'd made a mistake, but he wanted to do the right thing. "At this moment, I am really proud of you, son. Most boys your age would be very happy to walk away from this. And never look back."

Tom swallowed. "I—I'm not that great. I'd be happy to walk away from it, too."

"And that's why I'm proud of you. Because despite wanting to, you were instead willing to give up what you want most." She smiled at him. "Look, you go home. We'll call and see if we can get you a flight out of Santa Fe or Albuquerque today or tomorrow. Talk to Lucy. Tell her that we'll assume complete financial responsibility. I'll set something up where she'll have an assured monthly income until she's out of school and able to support herself. She'll have enough to live on, hire good child care and pay for the rest of her education. After that, we'll see. Okay?"

"Are you sure?"

Kate looked into her son's troubled eyes, and her heart hurt for him. He was sensitive and caring. That had been his downfall. That and those raging hormones, she amended wryly. "I'm very sure. You are not, repeat, *not* giving up college. Even if you *wanted* to marry Lucy, I'd still want you to go to school. Both of you."

Tom nodded, biting his lip.

"What?"

"I—I'll go see Dad while I'm home." He swallowed. "What do you think he'll say?"

Kate wanted to answer that Mark had made plenty of his own mistakes and, if he was upset, he certainly didn't have much room to talk. "Your dad will be upset at first, but he'll get over it."

Tom looked pained. "Everybody's gonna be talking about me now."

Kate shrugged. "Sticks and stones…"

"But don't *you* care? Cranbrook's a small town. Everybody'll know."

"No, I don't care. You haven't murdered anyone. You haven't cheated anyone out of their life savings. You haven't hurt anyone but yourself."

"And Lucy," he said glumly.

"She's just as responsible for this as you are," Kate reminded him.

He looked at her. "What would I do without you, Mom?"

She tightened her arm on his shoulder. "I hope you won't have to find out for a long, long time."

"But *why* is Tom going home?" Erin said. She'd been asking some variation of the question for the past hour, ever since Tom and Kate had returned to the motor coach.

"I told you, Erin. It's private business he has to take care of. When he wants you to know what it is, he'll tell you."

"But I—"

Kate closed the laptop. "Enough," she said. "He's going. End of story."

Erin's face darkened, but she didn't talk back. Instead, she turned around and said to Ginger, "Wanna go for a walk?"

Walk was the magic word to the dog, who immediately stood, tail whipping back and forth.

"Don't go too far," Kate warned automatically.

"Mom, I'm not a baby," Erin muttered.

Kate almost said *then don't act like one*, but decided it was unfair to take her anxiety over Tom's situation out on Erin.

When the screen door closed after Erin and Ginger, Kate sighed. Tom would be leaving in the morning. She had been able to secure him a seat on an eleven-thirty flight out of Albuquerque. He'd have to change planes in Houston, but would get into Austin around four-thirty in the afternoon, which wasn't bad. Right now he had walked outside to call Lucy and tell her he was coming. Tom also planned to call one of his buddies to see if he could pick him up.

"Are you gonna tell *me* what's going on?" Nicole said, walking out of the bedroom in her blue bikini. She and Tessa had decided to go swimming in the pool.

"No, I'm not."

Nicole blinked at the terse answer. "Tessa knows!"

"Did she say she did?"

"No, but you know she does. They tell each other everything."

Saving Kate from answering, Tessa emerged from the bathroom. She was also in a bikini, this one red and white stripes. "Ready?" she said to Nicole.

Nicole shrugged. "I guess."

Tessa's eyes met Kate's. "See you later."

Once they were gone, Kate buried her face in her arms. She felt incredibly tired, and even though she'd told Tom not to worry, that everything would be all right, she knew his life—all their lives—were going to change because of the coming baby. And even though she'd felt that little stir of anticipation earlier, she really wished this wasn't happening. Yes, she wanted grand-children someday, but she wanted them to come the way they were meant to come: to parents who were married and who loved each other.

Kate lifted her head at the creak of the metal screen door opening. "How'd it go?" she said to Tom.

He grimaced. "She's all excited. She wanted to come and pick me up at the airport, but I told her no."

"That's probably a good idea."

"Yeah, that's all I need. Her getting hysterical in the car or something. Not that I would have told her anything in the car, but Lucy's unpredictable. You never know when she's gonna lose it."

Kate shook her head. If only he'd broken off with her when he first wanted to. "Has she said how far along she is?"

"She told me she got pregnant in April, right before we broke up. When I asked how that could happen, since she was supposed to be on birth control pills, she said she kept forgetting to take them." This last was uttered in disgust.

Kate shook her head in disbelief. So careless. Kids always seemed to think they were immune from trouble. ""So she's only about two months along, then."

"I guess."

"Has she told her mother yet?"

"I don't know. She didn't say."

"What about her dad?"

"She's not close to her dad. She told me once she hadn't seen him in more than four years."

Once again, Kate thanked God for Mark. Okay, so he wasn't perfect or the greatest husband in the world, but he was a good father, and he did love his kids. He would never neglect them. "So who is going to pick you up?"

"Joey." Joey Milligan was Tom's best friend. Like Kate and Linda, the two boys had started school together in kindergarten and been fast friends ever since.

Suddenly Kate missed Linda desperately. They'd talked yesterday, but only for a short time. "I got you a seat on a flight tomorrow morning." She handed him the information, which she'd written on an index card. "I also transferred money into your checking account, so you should have more than enough to last you while you're there."

He nodded. "Mom…"

"What, honey?"

His eyes met hers. "Thank you."

The words sounded gruff, and she knew his emotions were raw. She got up and enfolded him in a fierce hug. Instantly, his arms came around her, too.

They stood that way a long while and, as Kate had thought hundreds of times before, she knew she would do anything in the world to protect her children. Even if the person she was protecting them against was themselves.

* * *

"Oh, Kate," Linda said. "Not Tom?"

"Yes, Tom."

"Poor kid. I tell you, I *never* liked that Lucy Robinson."

"I didn't know you knew her." Kate had never met Lucy.

"I know her mother. Cheryl. She comes here to exercise with the nine o'clock group."

"I thought she worked at the hospital."

"She does. The afternoon shift. Anyway, I've heard her talking to Betsy Hilliard. Complaining about Lucy, mostly."

"Why didn't you tell me?"

"I didn't want you to dislike the girl before even meeting her. I figured the romance might blow over, anyway, so what was the point? Besides, there's always two sides to every disagreement, right?"

"Right," Kate said. "But in this instance, looks like Lucy does have some serious problems. From what Tom told me, she's very emotional and clingy. Apparently he's been wanting to get away from her for months."

"Tom's too softhearted," Linda said loyally.

Kate smiled. Her steadfast loyalty was one of the things she loved best about Linda. If you were her friend, she would go through fire for you. Same for your kids. "I just hope the money didn't play a part in this."

"What do you mean?"

"I mean, I hope Lucy didn't get pregnant deliberately

because she knew about the money and saw it as her chance to get some of it."

"Shoot, I didn't even *think* of that. But you know, it sure makes sense. What better way to get a share?"

That damned money.

And yet…the money would ease Tom's way and enable him to still have his life, wouldn't it? Without the money, he'd have had to struggle for years to get an education and who knew if he'd ever have managed it?

They talked a long time and when Kate finally disconnected the call, she felt better.

Okay, so Tom had screwed up. But as she'd told him earlier, he hadn't committed a crime. He'd just made a mistake in judgment. And if a baby was the result, so be it.

It was nearly eight by the time Joey's Bronco sped past the Cranbrook city limits sign and twenty minutes after that before he pulled into the driveway of Tom's house.

Tom would never get used to the new house. Especially tonight he wished he was entering the familiar old house in their old neighborhood. "Hey, thanks, man," he said to Joey.

"Anytime, buddy." Joey made a face. "Good luck."

Tom sighed. "Yeah, thanks. I'll need it."

"Listen, don't back down."

"I won't."

"And don't worry. I'm not gonna tell anyone. I got my doubts she's really pregnant, anyway."

"I know you do. So does Tessa. But I know Lucy, and she sure sounded like she's telling the truth."

"You gonna call her tonight?"

"I told her I would. Hell, once I turn on my cell, I'm sure there'll be a message from her already." He laughed wryly. "That's how I avoid her. I keep my cell turned off."

"Hey, I would, too. That girl's scary."

Unfortunately, Tom agreed. And that's what scared *him*.

"Hey, you wanna go out for pizza tomorrow night?"

"Sounds good."

"Call me after you talk to her, okay?"

"It might be really late."

"So? You know me. I'm usually up till two."

"Okay."

Tom stood watching as Joey backed down the driveway, then waved as he drove off. Feet dragging, Tom hefted his duffel bag and walked around back.

Twenty minutes later, fresh out of reasons to put off making the call, he picked up the phone and pressed in Lucy's number.

CHAPTER 17

"Tom!" Lucy ran outside and flung herself at him.

It would have been mean to do what he wanted to do, which was push her away, so he simply stood there. But he didn't return her embrace because he knew if he did, she would just take that as a sign that he was coming back to her.

"Oh, Tom," she sobbed. "I'm so glad you're here. I just don't know what I would have done if you hadn't come."

Extricating himself, he said, "Let's go inside where we can talk."

"Oh. Okay." Her face was all puffy, as if she'd been crying for a long time.

His heart smote him, and yet—hadn't he *tried* to get away from her? Way *before* she got pregnant? And wasn't it her own fault she'd gotten pregnant in the first place? He wasn't the one who had forgotten to take his pills.

Inside, she started to lead the way into the living room, but Tom didn't want to sit in there. They'd had sex in there too many times.

"Let's go out to the kitchen," he said.

"But *why?*"

"Because we have a lot to talk about. A lot of decisions to make." *And I don't want you all over me....*

She sighed, but she followed him.

"Want a Dr Pepper?" she asked after he'd sat at the kitchen table.

"Sure." Having something to do with his hands would help him get through this. "Where's your mom?"

"She's working a double shift today."

"Have you told her yet?"

"What? About the baby?"

"Yes, about the baby."

Lucy shook her head. Her long blond hair was tied back in a ponytail today. Dispassionately, Tom studied her as she opened the fridge and removed the soft drink. Her curvy figure was outfitted in red shorts and a snug red-and-white striped T-shirt. There was no telltale bump in the front, but he guessed maybe two months was too soon for her to show.

"I wanted to get things settled between us first." She handed him the can of Dr Pepper, then sat opposite him. Her blue eyes held that innocent look he used to love. Now he knew the naiveté masked something darker.

"Well, I told *my* mom."

"You *did?*" She started to smile, but the smile faded at his expression.

"I wanted her to hear about it from me," Tom said. "I knew she'd be upset."

Lucy reached for the salt shaker, which sat on a lazy Susan in the middle of the table. She shook some of the salt into her hand, then licked it.

"Salt's bad for you," Tom said automatically, parroting something his mother had preached since he was little.

Lucy shrugged. "I like it."

Tom started to say it was probably bad for the baby, too. But what was the use? She wouldn't hear anything she didn't want to hear.

Instead, he opened the can of soda and drank some. He wished he was anywhere but there. But since he couldn't escape this, he wished he knew how to say he wasn't going to marry her without causing a scene.

"So what did your mom say?" Lucy asked.

She put the salt shaker back, and when she did, Tom could see her hand was shaking. He gulped more of the Dr Pepper. *Calm down. Just tell her....* "Like I thought, she was upset. You know, it's not the kind of thing you want to hear from your kid. I mean, she wants me to go to college."

Lucy put her hands in her lap. Her blue eyes pinned his. "Is she still mad?"

Tom shook his head. "No. In fact, she said she'd help you." He went on to explain what his mother had offered.

"But Tom...that's not what I want. I don't want to

be a single mother. I want us to get married and give our baby a real home."

He forced himself to meet her eyes. "I can't do that, Lucy."

Her bottom lip quivered.

"I'm sorry. I just…I can't be what you want." Hardening his heart, he added, "I don't love you. I told you that before."

"You *have* to marry me!"

He shook his head. "No. I don't. I know I have to support you financially, but that's *all* I have to do."

"This is your *baby*, Tom!" She pushed her chair back and stood. Pressing her palms against the table, she leaned forward. "You can't just walk away!"

"I'm not walking away. I told you. My mom is going to set you up financially and…after it's born, I'll…" He swallowed. "I'll be a part of its life."

"It! It! It! It's not an *it*, Tom. It's a *baby*! Your baby! You made this baby!" Each word shot out of her mouth like a bullet. "You were *happy* to make this baby. You couldn't get enough of me! But now you're *tired* of me. Tired! And you think you can just go away and forget about me!" Her eyes blazed, and spittle had gathered at the corners of her mouth. She looked crazy. For the first time ever, Tom was actually frightened of Lucy.

Sliding his own chair back, he stood up. "Look, maybe we should talk when you're not so upset.…"

"Where do you think you're going?" she shouted. "You aren't leaving!" Her chest was heaving.

"I—" He backed toward the doorway.

"You aren't leaving, you aren't leaving, you aren't leaving, you aren't leaving…"

Tom stared at her. What was wrong with her? Now she was tearing at her hair, all the while saying the same words over and over, running them together. His heart thumped painfully. He didn't know what to do.

She looked around wildly, then suddenly her hand darted out and yanked a knife out of the rack sitting on the counter behind her. Brandishing it like a weapon, she lunged toward him.

Tom did the only thing he could do. He whipped around and raced for the front door. Her feet pounded behind him. He barely managed to open the door and pull it shut behind him before she reached him. Her screams sounded like an animal in agony.

Using every bit of strength he possessed, with his left hand he held onto the handle, pulling it toward him so she couldn't open the door and with his right hand he reached into his pocket for his cell phone, struggling to flip it open and, using his thumb, pressed in the numbers 9-1-1.

Kate took her cell phone along with her when she walked Ginger. Tom had promised to call her after seeing Lucy this morning, and she didn't want to miss him.

She'd thought about him off and on all night as she tried to sleep. Maybe she should have gone with him. She could have left Tessa here to supervise. The girls would have been fine without her for a couple of days.

And yet…wasn't it best that Tom was handling this himself? After all, he certainly wasn't blameless in this affair. It took two to make a baby, and even though Lucy was supposed to be taking care of birth control, Tom should have been more cautious. Especially when he continued having sex with Lucy even after he knew he wanted to break up with her.

Kate sighed. Oh, who cared whose fault this was? Tom was her son. Her firstborn. She just wanted to protect him.

As she passed Gabe's coach, she saw him kneeling by the right front tire. He looked up. "Hey," he said.

"Hey, yourself." With difficulty, she wrenched her thoughts away from Tom. "Something wrong with your tire?"

"Nope. I just like to check them reguarly." He grinned at her. "You sore today?"

"Big-time." She couldn't help noticing how sexy Gabe looked this morning in his khaki shorts and snug-fitting black T-shirt. His gray-streaked brown hair shone with golden highlights in the sun. Everything about him looked healthy and fit.

"Isn't that Erin's job?" Rising, he inclined his head toward Ginger.

"The girls are cleaning the coach this morning."

"Voluntarily?"

"I bribed them," Kate admitted. "They wanted me to drive them into Santa Fe so they could get boots and riding apparel. It seems they all want to take riding lessons." She smiled ruefully. "I don't really want them to, but they wore me down. Anyway, I need to be here this morning, so that was our compromise. They'd stay here and clean the coach and after lunch I'd take them into town." She sighed. "I guess they'll start the lessons tomorrow."

"So they all fell in love with riding."

"Oh, Erin definitely did. As for Nicole and Tessa, I think the very cute Josh has something to do with *their* interest in lessons."

Gabe chuckled. "What about Tom? Is he halfway in love with Jenny?"

Kate's smile disappeared. She shook her head. "Tom's not here."

"Oh? Where'd he go?"

"Home."

"*Home?* Did something happen?"

Kate started to say Tom had some business that needed taking care of, but something about Gabe's expression made her want to confide in him. Walking to the picnic table between his coach and the one next to it, she sat down. He sat opposite her.

"What's wrong?" he said softly. His blue eyes held only concern.

She sighed for about the hundredth time since Tom had told her about Lucy. "Tom's former girlfriend called two days ago and informed him she's pregnant and he's the father."

Gabe grimaced.

"Anyway, he's gone back to Cranbrook to talk to her."

"You said it's his former girlfriend?"

Kate nodded. "They broke up in April, although he tells me he was trying to break up with her since the first of the year."

"Trying?"

"I know how it sounds, but Tom really is tender-hearted. And he's a true pacifist. He's always been like that. I'll never forget when he was about eight years old and we were at Mark's—my ex-husband's—company picnic. Another little boy about Tom's age was picking on him. Pushing him and calling him names, that kind of thing. And Tom just walked away. Tessa was the one who went after the other boy." Kate grinned. "She whacked him and kept whacking him. She hated when anyone did anything to hurt Tom. Anyway, that episode made Mark furious. He told Tom the other kid was a bully. He said it wasn't manly to let a girl fight his battles for him."

Kate hadn't thought about that scene in years, but now it came back in sharp detail. Tom's big eyes. The shame on his face as Mark berated him for being a sissy. Tessa's tears at her twin's unhappiness and how she'd glowered at her dad, even though normally she adored him. And Kate's own feeling of helplessness as she tried to derail Mark, who then got mad at *her*.

"Tom needs to learn how to defend himself," he'd insisted later, when she'd angrily told him *he* was the bully.

"Calling him names and making him feel as if there's something wrong with him isn't the way to do it."

Mark had given her a cold look. "Oh. So once again, you know best, right?"

Kate stared at him. "Maybe I don't know everything, Mark, but I do know you don't build a child's self-confidence and self-esteem by belittling him."

"Yeah, well, *I* know a boy can't survive in this world if he can't defend himself," Mark countered.

Had Mark been right? she wondered now. Had she done Tom a disservice by not trying to toughen him up as Mark had wanted?

"I was like Tom as a kid."

Kate blinked. She'd almost forgotten Gabe was there. *"You?"* she said in disbelief.

"Still am, to some extent."

"But—"

"But I look so macho, right?"

Kate smiled. "Just like the Marlboro Man in those ads."

"Inside I'm a marshmallow."

"Really." Kate didn't quite believe that. There was

something about Gabe that told her he would let no man push *him* around.

"That doesn't mean I wouldn't defend against someone trying to hurt me or mine, or that I wouldn't have moved heaven and earth to protect my son. I just mean I don't like fighting. I've never liked fighting. Some guys love nothing better than a good brawl. Not me. I prefer to use my brains instead of my fists. I think peace is preferable to chaos. And I despise people who take pleasure in hurting someone else."

I think I could fall in love with this man....

"I guess what I'm trying to say is, don't worry about Tom, Kate. He's a good kid. I could see that before we'd exchanged two sentences. He's sensitive and he doesn't like hurting people. There's nothing wrong with that." He smiled sympathetically. "He'll be okay. He made a mistake, yes, but hell, don't we all? And your ex-husband was wrong. Tom obviously knows which battles to walk away from and which he has to stand and face."

Some of Kate's anxiety melted at his words. Tom *would* be okay. No matter what happened this morning. She just wished the confrontation with Lucy was over soon and Tom would call, then she would be able to relax completely.

She smiled at Gabe. "Thank you. You've made me feel better."

"I'm glad," he said with an answering smile.

She got up. "I guess I'd better give Ginger that walk."

He nodded. "Oh, and Kate?" he added as she started to walk away. "If you want some help this afternoon in buying the girls their riding gear, I'll come with you."

"Seeing as how I know absolutely nothing about riding, that would be great."

"Albuquerque's a better place to go than Santa Fe, though. Cheaper prices. More selection."

"Oh, okay."

"Why don't you and the girls walk down when you're ready? I'll drive, if that's okay."

"You sure?"

"Yeah, my Land Rover is bigger and will hold more. In case we want to do some other shopping."

Kate said that was fine, then started down the roadway again to finish Ginger's walk. Half an hour later, as she turned and headed back to her coach, she still hadn't heard from Tom.

Tom couldn't get the picture of how the two cops had had to tackle Lucy to subdue her out of his mind. She'd screamed and screamed until the ambulance and the EMTs had come. After that, they'd taken her to the hospital.

Now Tom was sitting in the waiting area outside the emergency room. The nurse on duty had found Lucy's mom, who was with her now. Tom had answered all the questions and now he was just waiting to find out how Lucy was. He wished he could make the shaking in his stomach stop. He wanted to call his mom, but first he wanted to talk to Lucy's mom.

By now she probably knew about the baby. Tom had told the EMTs that Lucy was pregnant so they'd be careful and not give her anything or do anything that would hurt the baby. Tom cringed, thinking of what Cheryl Robinson was going to say to him.

Lost in his thoughts, he didn't notice the little girl standing in front of him. About six, she had big, dark eyes with long, curly eyelashes.

"Hi," she said.

Tom smiled. "Hi."

"Are you sick?" she said.

"Nope. Are you?"

She shook her head. "My mama's sick." She pointed past the others waiting to be seen to a young woman who was quietly moaning in the corner.

"My friend is sick," Tom said.

The little girl frowned. "Where is she?"

He inclined his head toward the door leading to the treatment rooms. "In there. The doctors are taking care of her."

"I wish—" But the child didn't finish the sentence, for just then the triage nurse called her mother's name, and she ran off.

Mother and child had barely disappeared into the inner sanctum when Tom saw Lucy's mother approaching. Tom swallowed at her stern expression.

She sat next to him, closed her eyes and expelled a heavy sigh. "The doctor said Lucy's delusional."

"Wh-what does that mean?"

"Basically that she doesn't see things as they are but as she wants them to be."

She went on to explain the details of the disorder. "They're afraid she'll harm herself or someone else. They're recommending putting her into a treatment facility. "

Tom digested this. "What about the baby?" he finally asked softly. "Will it be okay?"

Her head whipped around. "What baby?"

He wet his lips. "She...she's pregnant. I—I thought they would have told you. That...that's what we were...discussing when she got so upset. She wants me to marry her," he added in a rush, "and I told her I couldn't."

She just stared at him. "Lucy's not pregnant, Tom."

He blinked. "How...are you *sure?*"

"Of course I'm sure. I had to bring tampons home the other day because she was having her period. Believe me, she's *not* pregnant."

Tom's heart skipped. Not pregnant. Lucy wasn't pregnant. Had *never* been pregnant. It was all a lie. Relief made him feel weak. She wasn't pregnant!

"So she told you she was pregnant?" her mother asked wearily.

He nodded.

She bowed her head. "God, " she murmured.

Tom didn't know what to say. He felt bad for her. He could walk away now. But she never could. "I'm sorry," he finally said.

She looked up. Her blue eyes, so like Lucy's, met his. She nodded. "Yeah. Me, too."

"Mom?"

"Tom?" Kate's heart leaped at the sound of his voice. "How are you? How did it go?"

"I'll explain everything when I see you, okay? I'm coming back. I called Continental and I've got a seat on a flight tomorrow morning. Can you pick me up at the airport?"

"Of course, but Tom…is…is everything okay?"

"For me it is. Lucy's not pregnant. She never was."

Kate hadn't realized she was holding her breath until it escaped in a rush of relief.

"She's not okay, though. But like I said, I'll tell you all about it when I get there."

He gave her the information about the flight, and they said goodbye. Kate disconnected the call thoughtfully. So Lucy had never been pregnant. All that worry over nothing.

"Mom?"

Kate looked up to see Tessa standing there.

"Was that Tom?"

Kate nodded. "Lucy's not pregnant," she whispered.

Nicole was in the shower and Erin was in the bedroom changing into clean clothes in preparation for their shopping excursion, but Kate wasn't taking any chances on being overheard. There was definitely no reason for the two younger girls to ever know about this.

Tessa grinned. "Knew it. I just knew it."

Kate nodded, even though she hadn't been so sure.

"Is he coming home? I mean, back here?"

"Yes. In the morning."

Tessa's grin expanded. "*Okay*. So let's go buy some riding stuff, then!"

As the four of them walked down to Gabe's coach, Kate decided that maybe now she could finally relax and they could all have the wonderful summer she'd planned.

CHAPTER 18

The remainder of June seemed to fly by. The days were packed with activity. Every morning, early, all four children went off to the stables for their riding lessons. It didn't take long before the twins began to spend most of their time there hanging out with Josh and Jenny, to Nicole's intense chagrin and frustration.

"I hate her," she muttered one day as Tessa left the coach to go back to the stables.

"Hate who?" Kate said, coming out of the bathroom.

"Nobody," Nicole mumbled.

"You were talking about Tessa, weren't you?"

Nicole didn't answer.

Kate wanted to press the issue, even though she knew better. Jealousy between siblings was normal; she knew that. Hadn't she resented Joanna when *she* was a teenager? She contented herself with saying, "Do you want to go back to Cranbrook? I know your dad would love to have you stay with them until we get back." *As an unpaid babysitter....*

Nicole turned and glared at her. "No! Who said I wanted to *leave?*"

"Well, I just thought if you're unhappy…"

"I'm not unhappy!" And with that, she slammed out of the coach.

Give me strength, Kate thought, echoing one of her mother's favorite phrases as she and her sisters were growing up.

The day after this episode, in a stroke of luck, the couple occupying the site directly across from Kate's left, and less than two hours later, another coach arrived. Its occupants were a younger couple closer to Kate's age and they had two kids—a sixteen-year-old boy named Scott and a thirteen-year-old girl named Alexa.

Nicole took one look at Scott—a really gorgeous kid with jet-black hair, brown eyes and what Kate thought of as a killer smile—and all thoughts of the unattainable Josh sailed out of Nicole's mind. The icing on the cake was the fact Scott was a budding musician who played the guitar, wrote his own songs and could talk music for hours.

Erin, too, was thrilled with the newcomers. Soon she and Alexa were inseparable. And Kate liked the parents, Jim and Laurie O'Hara, although more and more, she spent her free time with Gabe.

They'd become fast friends. Underlying the friendship was an awareness, on both their parts, of the sexual attraction between them. But, to Kate's relief—she wasn't sure if she wasn't ready or if she was just plain scared—Gabe didn't act upon it, and neither did she. Even so, she knew if they continued to spend so much time together, sooner or later, something was bound to happen, because the chemistry between them couldn't be denied forever.

At the end of June, Kate had to decide whether to move on or stay at Juniper. That night, over dinner, she put the decision to a vote. It was unanimous. Everyone wanted to stay at the camp.

"You're sure you won't be sorry we didn't go to California?" Kate asked.

They all shook their heads.

"We love it here," Erin declared.

So Kate paid for the month of July and made a mental note to call Linda and ask her to find out exactly when Nicole and Erin had to be back at school.

Gabe smiled when she told him they were staying. "I've decided to stay, too," he said.

"I didn't know you were thinking of leaving," Kate said.

"I didn't want to," was his only answer.

Kate badly wanted to ask why, if he didn't want to, he had even considered it, but she suspected she knew. *Don't ask the question until you're ready to hear the answer....*

And so the first three weeks of July passed. It was an idyllic time. All of Kate's children were busy and happy.

No one there knew about the lottery so no one was badgering her. Kate reveled in the freedom from conflict, the lazy summer days and, most of all, her deepening friendship with Gabe.

Gabe.

Just thinking about him made her belly flutter.

Now, when they were together, the tension between them was almost palpable. And yet, as much as Kate wanted Gabe to make love to her, as much as she dreamed about it, she wasn't sure she could go through with it. What would be the point? The truth was, she liked him too much. So much that she knew she was already half in love with him. But it was a relationship that could go nowhere. Her life was in Cranbrook, with her children and her responsibilities. His wasn't. Without ever discussing it, she knew Gabe would never be happy there.

So, in essence, what they had was the equivalent of a shipboard romance. One that she could enjoy while it lasted, but would have to forget about afterward.

But if sex entered the picture, she might not be able to forget about it. She swallowed. She might get hurt. That was the bottom line. She might get hurt badly. Did she really want to take that chance? Was a night or two of sex—even wonderful sex—worth the pain that might follow?

The last week of July, Gabe said he wanted to take her to dinner in Santa Fe that Saturday night. "I thought we should have a special night out since we're both leaving next week."

"I'd like that," Kate said.

"Good. There's a great Italian restaurant there called Andiamo's. I'll call and see if I can get a reservation."

Kate was glad she'd brought along something pretty to wear—a favorite turquoise sundress and her strappy gold sandals. Just before leaving for the evening, she grabbed a lightweight cotton cardigan sweater out of the closet, because even in the heat of the summer, once the sun went down, the New Mexican night air could be chilly.

Gabe gave her an admiring glance when he saw her. "Don't you look nice."

He didn't look so bad himself in loose-fitting tan cotton trousers paired with an open-necked black knit shirt. For such a rugged-looking man, Gabe wore clothes well.

Shirley and Cindy were standing talking outside the DeSilvas' coach as they drove past. The two women grinned and waved. "Have fun," Cindy called out.

"We plan to," Gabe answered.

Kate couldn't help thinking about what Cindy had said to her the day before. The older woman had commented that both she and Shirley thought Kate and Gabe made a great couple. "You can tell how much he likes you," she'd added.

"I like him, too, but we're just friends," Kate had

answered. It wasn't really a lie. So far, they *were* just friends.

Cindy hadn't argued the point. Her knowing smile said it all.

As they left the RV park, Gabe gave her a sidelong glance and said, "I've been looking forward to this all day."

Kate's breath caught at his expression. "Me, too." *Oh, settle down. You'd think you were a teenager instead of a grown woman.* She was relieved when he put an Elvis Costello CD in the player.

It only took them forty minutes to get to Santa Fe and Andiamo's. Located in a modest house on Garfield Street in downtown Santa Fe, the restaurant was unassuming from the outside. In fact, Kate might have missed it if she'd been the one driving. Inside, though, it lived up to its billing as a neighborhood trattoria. It was filled with delicious smells, and the three dining rooms were packed with diners who all seemed to be having lively conversations over generously filled plates.

The food lived up to Gabe's promises. In fact, the crispy polenta appetizer Gabe ordered for them to share was so good, Kate could have made an entire meal of just that. By the time they finished their dessert—they split a lemon tart served with vanilla ice cream, again at Gabe's urging—Kate knew she'd have to eat very light for at least a week to make up for the way she'd stuffed herself tonight.

Twilight had settled over the city by the time they walked out of the restaurant and, as Kate had thought, the air was significantly cooler. She was glad she had her sweater in the car.

"Cold?" Gabe said, putting his arm around her shoulders.

Not now, she thought as warmth slid through her. She had the strongest urge to turn into his arms. It was all she could do to resist. When he removed his arm to help her up into the Land Rover, she felt bereft. *Oh, God, I want him…. I really, really want him….*

After he climbed into the driver's seat, he turned to her. "It's pretty early. You want to go for a drive? I'll show you the sights."

"I'd love that." Kate had been to Santa Fe several times, but hadn't really seen much of the city beyond the downtown area. Besides, maybe sightseeing would take her mind off sex with Gabe.

He drove through downtown, around the Plaza, then past St. Francis Cathedral. Pointing out landmarks along the way, he continued to Canyon Road where many of Santa Fe's art galleries were located, then cut over and drove along Alameda Drive and the river.

Kate thought the city was beautiful. The adobe homes fascinated her; they were so different from the brick she was used to at home. Idly, she wondered what it would be like to live there, where no one knew her and no one knew about the lottery. She fantasized about buying one of the houses. And if she lived in Santa Fe, maybe Gabe…

Oh, stop that. Gabe doesn't live here and he wouldn't move here simply because you were here….

Anyway, she'd never do it, because she couldn't leave Cranbrook. Even if she wanted to, how could she take the kids away from their father? She sighed.

"Why the sigh?" Gabe asked softly.

"*Was* I sighing?"

"You know you were."

Kate forced herself to smile. "Just woolgathering. Thinking about my family. My obligations."

By now they had left the busy street that paralleled the river and Gabe had turned onto a quiet residential side street. Once past the intersection, he pulled over close to the curb and parked. Turning to her, he said, "I've been thinking about this all night."

Kate's heart knocked painfully.

A moment later, she was in his arms.

The kiss ignited all the suppressed desire that had been building inside her from the moment she'd met him. So when he tore his mouth from hers, she actually felt a physical pain deep in her belly. Her heart was pounding so hard she was sure he could hear it.

His lips brushed her ear. "I want to make love to you, Kate."

She shivered. "I—" The word came out sounding like a croak.

His mouth captured hers again, his hand cupping her breast. When his thumb grazed her nipple, Kate sucked in a breath. Oh, God, that felt good. She had forgotten how wonderful it felt to be touched like this.

"Do you want that, too?"

"I…" She swallowed. "Yes," she whispered.

"But we can't do this here," he muttered. "We're not kids."

"W-we can't go back to the camp, either." There was no way she'd take a chance on the kids finding out, and they'd be sure to find out. The coaches were too close together. Someone would be sure to see Kate go into Gabe's.

"It's not even nine o'clock," he murmured against her hair. "Let's get a hotel room."

Kate thought of all the reasons she should say no. But now that she had to make a real choice, she didn't want to say no. So what if she got hurt? The only people who never got hurt were the ones who never took any chances. Did she really want to be one of those people? Then she thought about the kids and could feel herself wavering again.

"Call Tessa and tell her we've decided to go to the La Fonda Hotel and listen to music. That it'll probably be late when you get back and not to worry."

"How'd you know what I was thinking?"

She could feel his smile against her cheek. "Because I know you, Kate. You're a mother first, a woman second." He turned her face to his and looked into her eyes. "And that's one of the reasons I like you so much." Then he chuckled. "Of course, the other is, you're one damn sexy woman."

This time, his kiss was a promise of what was to come.

"Mom says she and Gabe are going to some hotel to listen to music and she'll probably be back late." Tessa snapped her cell shut, and her eyes met Tom's. The two of them were playing cards with Josh and Jenny at Josh's cabin.

Tom smiled. "Good. Hope she has fun."

Tessa hoped for more than that. She hoped Gabe fell in love with their mother. She'd been hoping that for a while now. "I told her I'd be back by midnight."

"I know. I heard you."

Tessa knew Tom wouldn't want to go back then. He always figured out a way to hang out alone with Jenny. And that suited her just fine.

"I'll walk you back when you're ready," Josh said.

Tessa smiled at him. She loved that he was willing to pretend they were just friends simply because she'd asked him to. Her feelings were too new. She just wasn't ready to share them, not even with Tom, although she knew he'd already guessed how things were.

Oh, she was so happy. Josh was the first real boyfriend she'd ever had, and he was so wonderful. Everything she'd ever hoped to find. It was going to be so hard to leave him. So hard to go off to Rhode Island to school. She wet her lips, pretended to study her cards. Without really thinking, she discarded one.

"Tessa, pay attention," Tom said.

Tessa blinked. "Sorry."

Maybe she wouldn't go....

Maybe she'd stay right there. It's what Josh wanted her to do. He was going back to Albuquerque after the summer was over. He already had a job lined up and he would be finishing up his bachelor's degree by taking night classes at the University of New Mexico.

"And you could go to the Art Center Design College," he'd said. "We could get a place together."

Her face felt hot.

God. She couldn't believe she was even *thinking* about doing this. What would her mother say? And RISD! The school had been her dream for so long. It was *the* school, the *best* school, for the career she hoped to have. How could she give it up?

And yet she knew she couldn't have both RISD *and* Josh.

She had to choose.

She swallowed. She'd only known Josh six weeks. Six weeks. Yet it felt like a lifetime. Remembering the night before, and what he'd said while they were making love, she shivered.

What was she going to do?

* * *

Nicole sighed. "Mom, I told you, we're *fine*. I'm watching a movie here with Scott, and Erin is over at the O'Haras' with Alexa. Her parents are there, too, so you don't have to worry." She looked over at Scott, who was sprawled on the couch in their coach. He grinned at her.

Nicole wished he wouldn't look at her like that when she was talking to her mother. She knew it was silly, but what if her mother guessed what the two of them had been doing when she called? Not that they'd been doing anything too bad. Just kissing…well, and touching each other. They didn't dare do anything else. Not here. What if Erin should come home? Or Scott's mother should walk over? They'd turned all the lights off—supposedly to watch the movie—so at least that nosy neighbor of theirs couldn't see them through the window. Nicole wouldn't put it past her to peek inside whenever she got the chance.

"Okay, then," her mother was saying. "Tessa said they'll be back by midnight, and I should be there no later than two."

"Have fun," Nicole said. She disconnected the call.

"So where were we?" Scott said in that sexy voice of his.

Smiling, Nicole walked toward him.

Gabe was a wonderful lover. It wasn't just that he was skillful—although he was—he was also thoughtful and generous. He wasn't in a hurry. He kissed her and touched her for a long time, paying minute attention to her body, finding all the places that gave her the most pleasure. Over and over, he told her how beautiful she was and how much he wanted her.

When he finally entered her, Kate had one of the most intense orgasms she'd ever had. It lasted so long, she had to bite her bottom lip to keep from crying out.

Afterwards, arms twined around each other, they talked quietly. He told her about his divorce two years after his son had been killed. "She couldn't stand being around me anymore," he said. "I just reminded her of Tony."

Kate's heart hurt for him.

"The marriage was shaky even before that, though," he admitted.

"Do you ever see her now?"

"No. She married again and now lives in Hawaii."

"What about you? Do you think about marrying again?"

"Sometimes. But up till now, I hadn't met anyone who interested me enough." He kissed her nose. "What do you say? Want to chuck it all and run off with me?"

Kate's heart skidded. "You're kidding, right?"

He didn't answer for a long moment. "I know you have responsibilities, Kate. So yeah, I guess I was kidding." He caressed her breast, then slowly, his hand moved lower. "But you don't know how much I wish we *could* go off together."

After that, they didn't talk again for a long time.

CHAPTER 19

As they drove back to the campsite, Kate realized something had happened to her tonight, something more than just the discovery that she was still desirable, that an attractive man could still find her beautiful and that she still had the ability to feel passion and to give and receive pleasure.

As they sped along the dark highway, a deep sense of peace and well-being filled her. Even the knowledge that she and the kids would be leaving New Mexico in just days and that she might never see Gabe again didn't shake that serenity.

I can handle this, she thought in wonder. *I'm not going to grieve if Gabe disappears from my life. My heart won't be broken. I can take this wonderful gift he's given me—the friendship, the respect, the terrific sex—without regrets. Even if I never see him again after this coming week....*

"Not sorry, are you?" he said softly.

"Not sorry at all."

Suddenly, Kate had a strong need to tell him about the lottery. "I know you've been wondering how I could afford our motor coach and the twins' college and quitting my job."

"Yeah, I have, but I figured it wasn't any of my business."

"I'd like to tell you." She told him about the way things had been before she'd won. She told him how thrilled she was when she *did* win and how she'd naively believed the money would solve all her problems. She told him what had happened afterward, how no one was happy with her, how they all wanted more and more.

Throughout, he listened quietly.

"I'm dreading going home again," she admitted when she was finished. "I'm so tired of all the conflict."

"You know, Kate, you can change things. You don't have to let the money continue to rule your life or dictate how you live."

"But how can I prevent it?"

"Same way I did. I got rid of most of my money." He went on to tell her he'd founded a large, very successful software company in the Silicon Valley that he'd eventually sold to a multinational corporation for an obscene amount of money. "At least it seemed obscene to me. After all, how many mansions can one person live in?" He smiled. "I don't even like mansions."

His disclosure didn't surprise Kate. Everything about him said he was a successful man. "So you gave it all away?"

"Not all. I made sure my parents would be well cared for, and I put aside enough for *my* old age, then I used most of the remainder to set up a foundation."

"Really? What kind of foundation?"

"Mainly it focuses on education, although part of the money is dedicated to medical research."

"Are you active in the foundation?"

"Nope. What do I know about running a foundation? I hired a professional. The point is, now I don't think about the money at all. I have enough to go another year or so without working, and after that, I'll find something else to do with the rest of my life. Something satisfying and hopefully…challenging." He smiled at her. "I like a challenge."

She smiled, too. "No surprise there."

"I'm telling you, Kate, you wouldn't believe how freeing it is not to have to worry about the money."

"But won't you miss it? I mean, you're used to fine things."

"Nope. I've discovered I don't need much to be happy."

Kate thought about what he'd said for the remainder of the drive back and was still thinking about it the next morning. And the more she thought about it, the more sense it made.

She *had* been letting the money dictate how she lived. And that was ridiculous. Money was a tool, simply a means to an end, and it should never be allowed to become more.

She began to wonder if she could do something similar to what Gabe had done. Certainly she had to do something. This summer away from Cranbrook had been a wonderful respite.

But soon she would go back to her real life. And if that life wasn't to continue in the same vein as when she'd left Cranbrook, she would need to make some tough decisions.

"I'm sorry, Josh." Tessa blinked back tears. "I'm afraid if I give up RISD, I'll always be sorry."

"You don't love me. Why don't you just say it?"

Tessa could feel herself weakening at the hurt on his face. "Josh, please try to understand. I think I *do* love you, but I'm only nineteen. I—I think about what happened to Tom and how he very nearly ruined his life, and I—I don't want that to happen to me."

He turned away. "Go then."

She touched his arm. "Josh … "

He shook it off. "Just go, okay?"

Now the tears *did* fall. "Please, Josh. Please don't do this. This doesn't have to be the end for us. We can talk every day. We can e-mail and text message. I can come and see you, and you can come and see me. And if we still feel the same way about each other next year, I'll come and spend the summer with you."

But he wouldn't look at her.

Once again, Tessa almost changed her mind. What

if she never found anyone like Josh again? What if this was her one chance at real love and she was throwing it away? And yet, deep in her heart, she knew she wasn't ready to make this kind of commitment to anyone.

She cried all the way back to the camp.

Tom couldn't wait to get home. The summer had been great—especially once the situation with Lucy had been resolved—but he was ready to begin the rest of his life. Columbia had turned him down, but that was okay. He had decided on Texas A&M and was anxious to get to College Station, find an apartment and get settled.

All that was left was saying goodbye to Jenny.

He smiled. Jenny was a terrific girl. So far they were just friends, but he knew they could be more. They'd already made plans for her to come and visit him over Thanksgiving.

And after that, who knew?

Whistling, he set off for the stables.

"Come on, Nicole, you're bein' a tease."

Nicole shook her head. She and Scott were deep in the woods, in this little clearing they'd found. They'd come here often in the past weeks to make out.

"You're probably the only sixteen-year-old virgin in your class," Scott said derisively.

"I'm not sixteen yet."

"Whatever."

Nicole probably *was* the only virgin in her class. But was that a *bad* thing?

"I thought you really liked me," Scott said.

Now he was giving her that look, the one that made her stomach feel all funny inside. "I do. But—"

"What?"

"I just…" She shook her head again. "I can't explain it. I—I just can't." The truth was, she was scared. Although she loved it when he kissed her and touched her, and she loved kissing him and touching him, she was afraid if they went all the way she'd be just like Tracy and some of the other girls she knew and want sex all the time.

"Okay, fine. Who cares, anyway?" Angry now, he stalked off toward the lake.

Nicole almost ran after him.

But she didn't.

Instead, head hanging dejectedly, she walked slowly back to the coach.

Erin cried as she kissed Pepper goodbye. She would miss her horse so much. Oh, she knew Pepper wasn't *really* her horse, but she felt like her horse.

"Bye," she whispered. "I'll miss you."

Pepper nickered softly.

Erin reached into the pocket of her shorts and took out the plastic bag of cut-up apple. Feeding the treat to the horse, she continued to tell Pepper how much she loved her. "Even if I get a horse of my own, I'll never forget you," she said fiercely.

As she walked back to camp, Erin vowed that somehow, some day, she'd see Pepper again.

Kate said her goodbyes, saving Gabe for last.

In the privacy of his coach—she was past caring what anyone might think—they kissed.

"God, I'll miss you," he said.

Kate smiled through her tears. "I'll miss you, too."

"I want you to know, Kate, that meeting you is one of the best things that's happened to me in a long time."

"I feel the same way."

He kissed her again, his lips lingering. "I don't want to say goodbye."

"I don't, either."

Nuzzling her ear, he whispered, "You know, I've always wondered what Christmas in Texas would be like."

Kate drew back to look at him. "Why don't you come and find out?"

"I might do that. I just might do that."

And then he kissed her again.

Kate and the kids talked all the way home. She told them what she'd been thinking and they discussed the situation thoroughly. She'd been afraid they would be disappointed or unhappy with the things she wanted to do, but they were surprisingly supportive, especially after Kate told them there would still be enough money for Erin to have a horse and continue her riding lessons and for Nicole to get the expensive violin she coveted and for the twins to live independently the next four years.

So after they arrived home August 4, Kate began to implement her plan. The first thing she did was put the new house up for sale. As soon as it sold, she planned to buy a house in their old neighborhood.

The second thing she did was call a meeting with her sisters and mother. She told them that the money she'd won had caused too many problems between them.

"So here's what I've decided," she said. "I'm giving each of you $700,000. I thought about buying you an annuity instead, but then I decided you should have the chance to make your own decisions about your future. Personally, I hope you'll invest this money, but if you prefer to spend it or give it away, that's your choice."

"And that's *it?*" Joanna said, incredulous. "Why, your new house cost that much!"

"I'm selling the house," Kate said. "I hate it. And no, that's not all. I'm also establishing college funds for your children. If they don't want to go to college, the money will remain in their funds until they reach the age of thirty. After that, they can use it any way they want to."

Joanna's mouth opened, then closed again.

"Are you doing the same thing for *your* kids?" Mel asked angrily.

"Yes." That had been a hard decision for Kate, but she knew it was the right one. It would be no kindness to give her kids too much money. They deserved the privilege of earning their own way in the world. As it was, they had far more than most kids had. Far, *far* more.

And the third thing Kate did was establish a foundation called The Good Samaritan, which would help single mothers who were struggling the way she had struggled. She planned to run the foundation herself. Unlike Gabe, its goals interested her, and she felt she had a lot to offer. Besides, what she didn't know, she could learn.

She ignored the continued grumbling of her sisters. *They'll get over it*, she thought. *And if they don't, that's their problem, not mine.*

Her mother, however, actually seemed to approve what Kate was doing, which pleased Kate enormously. Maybe there was hope for their relationship yet.

Kate had enlisted the help of both Keith and Adam to set up the foundation. Much to her surprise, both men seemed to admire her decision and both ended up asking her out again.

Wasn't life funny? she mused after a long conversation with Gabe where she'd brought him up to date on everything she'd done since they'd been home.

In less than a year, she had gone from being a woman who was living hand to mouth and worrying constantly about money to a woman whose financial future was secure and who was now in a position to help others. But most amazingly of all, she'd gone from being a woman with no energy or time for dating—much less anyone who was interested in her—to being a woman who had not one, not two, but three attractive men in her life.

Kate grinned.

At this rate, she could hardly wait to see what might happen next.

* * * * *

*Turn the page for a sneak preview of
Merline Lovelace's EX MARKS THE SPOT,
coming to NEXT this April.*

"You're going gray, Armstrong."

"Are you just now noticing?"

Fascinated by those errant strands, she ran her fingers through the short, thick layers.

"I'm glad I'm not the only one showing signs of age."

"Now that you mention it," he said with a slow smile, "I have noticed a few wrinkles. They look good."

His glance drifted over her face and snagged at her jawline. His smile fading, he traced the small white scar with his thumb.

"This from the IED?"

"Yes."

"I didn't learn you were in that marketplace until two days after the explosion."

She shrugged aside the implied accusation. "I wasn't hurt. All I got was this little scratch."

"And the bacteria that slipped into your blood through the open wound."

"And that."

As his calloused pad feathered over her skin, it

occurred to Andi they were alone in the empty shop, nested together like Russian dolls.

The same thought must have occurred to Dave. His thumb stilled. The air seemed to get heavy around them.

Andi sensed his intent a second or two before he leaned into her. Her pulse skipping and stuttering, she splayed a hand against his chest.

"Wait."

"For what?"

"This...this isn't smart."

"Maybe not," he murmured, his mouth a mere inch or two from hers. "Then again, it could be the smartest thing we've done in years."

When your life comes unraveled, cast on and start over!

Libby Cartwright never planned on inheriting a yarn shop from her estranged mother. But now, running Metropolitan Knits means Libby has lots to learn about knitting, motherhood and even romance. As the grand reopening approaches, Libby learns to knit two together— in knitting and in life....

Knit Two Together

Connie Lane

Available March 2007
TheNextNovel.com

HN80

HARLEQUIN®
Next™

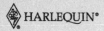

Romantic
SUSPENSE

*Excitement, danger
and passion guaranteed!*

USA TODAY bestselling author
Marie Ferrarella
is back with the second installment
in her popular miniseries,
*The Doctors Pulaski: Medicine
just got more interesting...*
DIAGNOSIS: DANGER is on sale
April 2007 from Silhouette®
Romantic Suspense (formerly
Silhouette Intimate Moments).

*Look for it wherever
you buy books!*

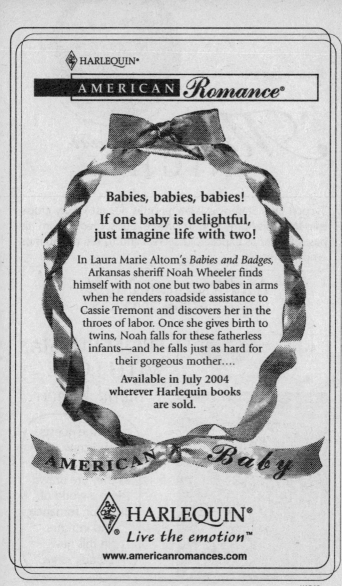

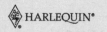

HARLEQUIN®

Mediterranean NIGHTS™

Tycoon Elias Stamos is launching his newest luxury cruise ship from his home port in Greece. But someone from his past is eager to expose old secrets and to see the Stamos empire crumble.

Mediterranean Nights
launches in June 2007 with...

FROM RUSSIA, WITH LOVE
by *Ingrid Weaver*

Join the guests and crew of *Alexandra's Dream* as they are drawn into a world of glamour, romance and intrigue in this new 12-book series.